EVERYTHING

KING'S DAUGHTER'S STORY COLLECTION #2

CONTENTS

EVERYTHING
BY JAE FISHER

A NEW CHAPTER.
A new beginning.

I started this chapter,
Knowing I might not finish.
I opened this door
Knowing that it might be shut.

But whatever I do,
It is for a purpose
That is beyond my control.

The purpose is a purpose that
Was set before me
Even before I was born.

He is my everything:
Dedicating every word
To the purpose.

The purpose will bring Him glory
Throughout my days.

EVERYTHING
BY BREE PEMBROOK

Everything Works Together

"TAKE THIS, LITTLE one," the baker's wife said to the street boy, Sam, who stood on tiptoes, peering at the fresh bread loaves that covered the counter. She handed him a big brown loaf. "It will be my gift to you."

He thanked the kind lady and ran out onto the streets of Bristol before the grumpy baker, who didn't like street rats, could return and find out what his wife had done.

When he knew no one saw, he settled down beside a garbage pail in a dark alley, where the morning rays didn't yet peek over the buildings. Sam gazed lovingly at the warm loaf before biting through the thick crust. A rare treat. Sam carefully stashed the rest in his capacious pocket. He trotted farther down the alley.

So far today, everything was going splendidly. He had slept well and uninterrupted the night before, and now he had enough food to last for a few days. What could be better?

Mr. Müller, the man who ran the mission Sam visited, always said how everything worked for the good of those who love the Lord, and everything was working out wonderfully for this Lord-loving boy. He skipped to a stop at the edge of the street.

Happening to look down at his feet, Sam saw a shilling shining up at him from the sidewalk. Better and better! He scooped it up and dropped it into his other pocket. Now it was time to go to Mr. Müller's place and have some more breakfast!

The boy sped up, dodging the few people on the street. Suddenly, he was knocked into the brick wall of a dress shop. Another bigger, mean street boy was holding him there.

"Empty your pockets!" he demanded. When the boy made no move to do so, the bully thrust his hand into one pocket, then the other. He withdrew the precious shilling. "Ha!" The boy gave Sam one final shove and hurried down the street.

The robbed boy sighed. His shilling was gone. He was surprised the boy didn't steal his bread as well. Sam felt his pockets and found out why; the loaf was gone! He dug deeper and felt no bottom in it. How could he have forgotten that the entire bottom of that pocket had fallen apart? Now he had nothing. The day he had thought was so wonderful was getting worse and worse. Backtracking down the street, he searched for his bread. He found it squashed to a paste by carriage wheels.

Sam slowly continued down the sidewalk. Finally, with empty pockets, he made it to Mr. Müller's home. He hurried into the dining room.

"Ah, welcome, Sam," Mr. Müller said. "Please, be seated. We are just about to bless our meal."

As he sat down, Sam glanced around, then stared at his empty plate. Where was the food? There wasn't a crumb in sight! The other children around him seemed worried too. Maybe Mr. Müller was wrong about things working together for good for them.

Mr. Müller noticed the confusion on Sam's and the rest of the children's faces. "My God is not limited. He can again provide," he said.

Sam fingered the pocket he had put his bread in, imagining the wonderfully warm loaf, trying to take his mind off of his growling stomach.

"Lord," Mr. Müller began, silencing Sam's thoughts, "we know that everything works for the good of those who love You. And now, Lord, we ask that You would give us the food we need to have strength for today."

A knock at the door interrupted the prayer. Mrs. Müller opened it to the baker—the very one that hated the poor thieving street children.

"God put it into my mind to bring you some bread," he said, revealing a huge tray of dark brown loaves. "I have more in the wagon."

Mr. Müller beamed, looked up as though saying a silent prayer of thanksgiving, and took the tray from the baker willingly. He began distributing the bread to each of the three hundred children, including Sam.

"Thank you very much, sir, and God bless," Mr. Müller called as the baker strode back to his wagon after unloading the last of the bread.

Almost as soon as Mrs. Müller closed the door, another knock sounded on it. With a knowing smile, Mrs. Müller opened the door again.

There the milkman stood, a crate of milk under each arm. "Me wagon wheel broke jus' outside yer place. The milk shall go bad waitin' fer the wheel to be fixed, so I thought to meself, mebbe the orf'ns could put it t' good use." He set the crates just inside the doorway and went back for more.

"God is truly blessing us," Mr. Müller said as he

followed to help the milkman. "Everything is working together for us, as He has promised."

Sam wondered about that. He was blessing them now, but how come He had let Sam's shilling be taken and his bread get lost? Sam thought about what his shilling would have bought. Perhaps a scone, a wooden top, maybe even candy!

As the milkman left to find someone to fix his wagon, Mr. and Mrs. Müller poured glasses of milk for each child.

Sam bit into the bread he was given and sipped his milk.

After the meal, Mr. Müller pulled Sam aside. "I'd nearly forgotten that you still do not have a roof over your head or a bed to call your own," he said. "If you hadn't been late, I would never have remembered. One of the children has moved to his uncle's house. Would you like to live here now that there's room?" Mr. Müller smiled when he saw Sam's beaming face. "That's the only time I will believe being late is good, Sam." He ruffled the boy's hair.

"May I? Honest?" Sam was shocked. He hadn't even thought about the possibility of staying in Mr. Müller's orphanage, but now the opportunity was right in front of him.

"Of course. We'll get you all settled this afternoon."

"Thank you, thank you, Mr. Müller!" Sam exclaimed as he skipped out the door.

As he walked back to the alley that used to be his home, he thought. If he hadn't had his shilling taken from him and lost his bread, he would have been on time, but because he had been stopped by the bully and spent some time looking around for his food, he was late. Because he was late, he jogged Mr. Müller's memory. Now, he had a home! Sam clicked his heels with joy. Mr. Müller was right.

Everything was working out for those who love God! Everything worked together for Sam, His newest follower, and everything was perfect.

EVERYTHING
BY ANALISE M. MARTIN

I'M HOME NOW. And everything has changed. The house is freshly painted and every room is filled with people I have grown to know and love. When one is called away, another quickly takes their place. And that is how it should be. There are always fond memories of those who have been here, and we are always making new memories with those who remain.

There is an orchard on one side of the lane now, just starting to come into its legacy of rich-hued apples. I guess you'll reap the full benefits of it, which is as it should be. I want to leave everything to you, my child in spirit if not by blood. I don't know you yet, and maybe I never will. But God will direct me when the time comes, and I will leave you everything. Oh, I know, it's not going to make you rich. But it will feed you with all the rich foods of a life surrounded by beauty and lovers of beauty.

It might take you a while to embrace this calling that God has laid on my heart for you. But He will give you the assurance of it, and you will come home just as I did.

I pray for you daily, that you would grow strong in Him, that you would learn from these letters, written by a humble pen, something of use to you. I can't help but write them, but what I can do is try to capture an honest thought or two and give them to you with my heart full of love. There is so much love here that it covers multitude after multitude of sins. Every person who enters these doors feels their burdens lighten. And that is as it should be.

You, my child, will have much to learn when you come here. Let these friends teach you their wisdom. It is more than I will ever know, but I want it. Oh, I want it desperately.

I've been realizing how much I lack in wisdom and love in the last weeks. It takes a very gentle hand to deal with my sins. A very insistent one too. Thank the Lord that He is both of those things, above all that I could ever imagine.

Dear child, I've been writing this letter over the past several weeks, as the house bustles around me. I bustle right along with it most of the time, but I need my quiet time alone. And so I retreat to my porch even though it is nearly winter. The glass isn't very good insulation, but I have a heater and it does quite a good job of keeping me toasty. One of Opa's sketches hangs on the wall now. It's unfinished, which is why it isn't hung in the house. I put it away for a long, long time. But now I want the reminder that he is watching me from up there in heaven, laughing when I laugh, loving every second of this life that he created for me and wanted me to create for others. How could he have known that this house and the people inside it would become everything to me. My life, my love, my joy. I am indeed blessed beyond measure!

I wonder if he knew when he asked me that how much of the creation would come from those who came to enjoy it. I in myself can do nothing. I in God can do something. But I in God with others in God? We can do more than I would have ever dreamed to hope.

There is a woman sitting on the lawn, head bent

backwards as she gazes upward. I think she's seeing God in the blueness of the sky. She sits there for hours every day, her mouth slowly moving, conversing with Him. Her husband goes for long, long walks by himself, often bringing home another child who needs a good hot meal. He offers to pay for it, and I refuse. Every time. He doesn't want to impose on my hospitality, and he has no right, but the child looks so lost, and he has so much. I gently assure him that the child is welcome at our table and that he is perfectly within his rights bringing him here.

The man who is slowly marching through the flower gardens—he came home from India three years ago. His son is carrying on his ministry, and our friend has nothing to do but wait, seek the Lord, and pray for the ministry that he has passed into younger hands.

Those two teenage girls walking out the lane—they will leave next week for extended mission trips. One of them is going to Indonesia, one to Peru. We will sing them out the lane with that old blessing song. *May the road rise to meet you, may the wind be at your back, may the sun shine warm upon your face, may the rain fall softly on your fields, and until we meet again, may you keep safe in the gentle, loving arms of God.* I think I will leave you, for this time, with that. It says better than I could what I wish for you.

Your loving parent in Christ,
Marie

EVERYTHING
BY P.D. ATKERSON

GREGORY WAS YANKED from the blissfulness of sleep when forty-five pounds of pure energy landed on top of him. With a grunt, Gregory opened his eyes to find another face mere inches from his own.

"Is the house on fire?" he muttered, frowning at his son, who shook his head. "Is there someone trying to kill you?" When he received a "nope" in response, Gregory raised an eyebrow at him. "Then what could possibly have you out of bed at…five in the morning?"

Pouting, Winnie rolled over and onto the bed beside him. "Wow…you really are old if you don't remember what today is," he said, grinning up at Gregory as he kicked against the bed. "How old are you now? Ninety?"

"Oh, yeah?" Gregory said, raising an eyebrow as he reached out and started tickling him.

Winnie let out a shriek as he tried to pull away, but Gregory just hooked his arm around his son's chest and held him firmly. "Now, why does *my* birthday have you up so early?" he asked before blowing against Winnie's neck.

Winnie giggled and tried to pull away. "Duh. Because you always made chocolate chip pancakes for *my* birthday, you should definitely do it for yours. I'll even eat them all for you."

"All right, you little monster," Gregory scoffed, swinging Winnie over him and depositing him onto the ground beside his bed. "Now, get out of here while I get dressed, or I'll have *you* for breakfast."

Sticking out his tongue, Winnie darted out of his room.

Shaking his head, Gregory chuckled to himself as he shoved back the covers and climbed out of bed. He was not looking forward to Winnie's teenage years. With that slightly unsettling thought, he made his way to his closet and quickly got dressed.

Five minutes later he made his way downstairs, hoping the silence of the house wasn't a bad sign.

"Winnie?" he called, heading toward the kitchen. "You'd better not be eating those chocolate chips by themselves!" He stepped through the doorway, and Winnie shot him a grin from where he was sitting on one of the stools.

"Daddy," Winnie said, placing his hand over his heart. "I would *never*…do that when I know you're coming down."

Gregory just rolled his eyes as he made his way toward the fridge and started preparing everything he needed for the pancakes.

It was hard to believe that it had already been over ten years since the first time he'd had pancakes, and he'd lost track of how many times he'd had them since.

He wasn't surprised that Winnie only made it through him making two pancakes before he scrambled off to go play.

Twenty minutes later, Gregory was finished and just about to call Winnie when his phone buzzed on the counter beside him.

Stifling the sigh that tried to escape him, he turned

off the heat on the last pancake and picked up the phone.

He wished he was surprised to see it was Mitch.

Gregory hit "answer" and held it up to his ear. "What is it this time?" he muttered, pinching the bridge of his nose.

"A potential bomber at a political rally here at the Capital," Mitch said, sounding more tired than he had been the last time they'd talked.

A *"potential bomber,"* Gregory thought, grimacing to himself as he moved to scramble the now burned pancake out of the pan. *Happy birthday to me.* "When do I need to leave?" he asked.

"In the next ten minutes would be ideal," his handler said. "I've already got an agent headed your way. She should be there soon, and then it's about a twenty-minute drive, if you go the speed limit."

"Understood," Gregory said, gritting his teeth before he hung up the phone and shoved it into his pocket. "Winnie! I need you in here now, Kiddo," he called as he grabbed a couple of pancakes and tossed them on a plate.

A second later, Winnie stepped into the kitchen, not exactly pouting, but close enough. "You have to go, don't you?" he whispered, glaring at the ground.

Gregory sighed, tossing the plate of pancakes onto the table before he stepped toward Winnie and knelt down. "Yeah, I do. But I promise I'll be back as soon as I can, then we'll spend the rest of the day together. How does that sound?"

"Okay," Winnie said, sighing. "Just... be careful."

"I always am," Gregory said, grinning as he stood up, even if he didn't exactly feel it.

He hated the fact that Winnie seemed to have expected this to happen. He'd always gone on a lot of missions, but ever since his son had been born, the time between missions seemed to be annoyingly small.

"All right." Gregory clapped his hands together and nodded toward the table. "Eat the pancakes while they're still hot. An agent should be here soon to watch you, and I've got to get ready."

He got a nod in response as Winnie stepped toward the table and scrambled up onto his seat before he started to eat.

Thankfully, he'd finished getting ready by the time Agent Fletcher arrived.

After comparing her badge to what Mitch had sent him, Gregory quickly ushered her inside and introduced her to Winnie.

"Nice to meet you," she said, giving him a polite smile, which Winnie did not return.

Gregory grimaced before squatting down in front of his son. "Behave for her," he whispered, kissing him on the top of the head before he stood up and ruffled Winnie's hair. "I'll be back for dinner. Promise."

Even if he had to leave the mission unfinished, he wasn't going to disappoint his son.

"Don't worry about us, Agent Winfield," Fletcher said, smirking as she placed her hand on Winnie's shoulder and draped her arm over his head.

Gregory was pretty sure she wouldn't be doing that if she could see the murderous look Winnie was shooting her way.

"Right," Gregory said, doing his best to give Winnie a reassuring smile as he stepped through the door and headed toward his car.

As it turned out, Mitch was right about how long it would take him to get to the rally, and twenty minutes after leaving the house, Gregory found himself illegally parking in front of the venue.

He wasn't about to waste time finding a parking space, then trudging all the way back to the front door.

There were some advantages to his job.

"Give me the breakdown," he said, skipping the pleasantries as he moved to fall into step beside his handler as they headed into the venue.

"We've isolated the suspect away from the civilians," Mitch said, ushering Gregory into an office they'd obviously commandeered. "We decided to wait for you before doing anything else."

Gregory nodded. "Well, let's get started then."

It didn't take him long to decide that Uncle Sam had set this whole thing up to try to ruin his birthday. He was pretty sure the local PD could have handled it, especially since that was what SWAT was for.

Then again, his rate on the weekends was probably cheaper.

And that's exactly what he told Mitch, once they'd wrapped things up and were headed to their waiting vehicles. "I feel like I'm used like duct tape and WD-40. Whenever Uncle Sam has a problem, no matter the size, he throws me at it," Gregory said. "Seriously, does the man have nothing better to do with his time than manipulate my life?" Gregory huffed, rubbing at his temples as he moved to open his car door.

"After all these years, do you actually still believe I have any idea what goes on inside that man's head?" Mitch asked, raising an eyebrow at Gregory. "I'm just following orders too. In fact, he hardly ever gives them to me in person anymore."

You know what? Gregory wasn't in the mood to play this game. "Whatever," he said, yanking the car door open.

"He's been the same for the past ten years; I don't imagine he'll change any time soon."

Gregory didn't wait to find out if Mitch had anything to say to that before he climbed into his car and closed the door behind him. Then he took a second to cool off before starting the car and heading back home.

At least it was only a couple of hours and not the whole day wasted on a mission he was pretty sure anyone else there could have taken care of.

And here he'd thought it was different on this side of the law, but it would seem both sides of the game needed pawns, and he was apparently a natural. "God, I don't know what I'm doing anymore," he whispered.

Things used to be different when he was younger. He used to feel like he was actually doing some good. But now… It felt like all he was doing was fighting fire with fire.

He was losing those he loved and a part of himself along the way.

It felt like he was always choosing between his job and those he loved. He barely spoke to his parents anymore. The only time he interacted with *some* of his siblings was on holidays or when Jackson and Frank's jobs somehow intersected with his own.

And then there was his wife.

The woman who'd walked out on him when he wasn't even there, leaving him with their three-year-old son to raise alone.

He pulled up to his driveway and parked the car, blowing out a breath as he closed his eyes. "I feel like I'm just spinning my wheels while everything spirals out of control," he prayed. "I don't even know if I'm doing what You want me to do anymore. But please, just show me what to do." He sighed, knocking his head back against the headrest as he opened his eyes again.

He was pretty sure most twenty-four-year-olds didn't start having a mid-life crisis on their birthday.

Shaking away that thought, Gregory unbuckled and climbed out of the car.

When he reached the house, he was slightly irritated to find that the front door was unlocked and he didn't even have to use his key to get in.

He quietly opened the door and slipped into the house. It only took him a second to hear someone talking in the living room.

But he didn't hear Winnie's voice.

Fighting the urge to draw his gun, Gregory made his way into the living room, and when he stepped inside the room, he was glad he hadn't pulled his gun. But at the same time, he wished he had.

"What the heck is going on here?!" he snapped at Agent Fletcher, who was practically sitting on the lap of a man Gregory had never seen before.

Fletcher scrambled away from the man so fast that Gregory was surprised she didn't fall on her face.

"Agent Winfield! I… I wasn't expecting you back so soon," she stammered, scrambling to her feet as she quickly straightened her suit. But at the moment, Gregory wasn't interested in her, or even her boyfriend.

He was far more interested in the person who *wasn't* there.

"Where is Winnie?" he asked, narrowing his eyes as he glared at the woman.

Agent Fletcher blushed as she crossed her arms and seemed to try to look unbothered by the whole thing. "I uh… I sent him up to his room. He's fine."

"You…" Gregory blew out a breath. "Did you at

least check to make sure he actually went to his room, and that he's *fine*?" The guilty look he received in response was all the answer he needed. "Get out. Now. Or I might do more than just write you up, *Agent* Fletcher."

The color drained from the woman's face a second before she scrambled to get her things, grabbed her boyfriend's arm, and fumbled to exit as quickly as possible.

As he locked the door behind them, Gregory fought the urge to punch something.

Apparently even a full-fledged agent could be just as bad of a babysitter as a high schooler.

The next person Gregory left Winnie alone with was getting a full background check.

Running his hand through his hair, Gregory pulled off his jacket and was just about to head upstairs to check on Winnie when there came a *crash!* from the kitchen.

Instantly, Gregory whipped his gun out and started toward the kitchen. He was only a few yards away when he got a whiff of something burning. He stepped into the kitchen, and he could honestly say what he found was not what he was expecting.

"Winnie?" he said, and his son let out a small squeak as he whipped around toward him.

"Daddy! I didn't expect you to be home yet!"

Gregory raised an eyebrow and glanced around the mess that had in a past life been a kitchen. "I can see that."

The counter and the floor were coated in powder and dirty dishes. Smoke poured from the oven, and Winnie! Winnie was *covered* in what Gregory could only hope was chocolate frosting.

"What's going on here, Kiddo?" he asked, stepping around an overturned bowl and several utensils as he moved to turn the oven off.

Gregory wasn't expecting to turn around again to find Winnie on the verge of tears. "Hey!" Gregory said, kicking some eggshells and another bowl out of the way as he knelt in front of his son. "What's wrong, sweetheart?"

"I'm sorry," Winnie cried, no longer holding back his tears. "I tried to get Fletcher to help me, but she called it 'stupid' and sent me to my room. I... I thought I could do it on my own, but—but all I did was ruin it! I'm sorry, Daddy."

Gregory was very confused. "If you wanted to bake something, you should have just waited until I got home, and I would have helped you, Kiddo. You know there's nothing I wouldn't do for you."

For some reason that just seemed to make Winnie cry worse. "It was supposed to be a surprise!" Winnie said, kicking one of the plastic bowls away from him. "I was going to give the cake to you tonight as a birthday gift. But I ruined it, and I made a mess of the kitchen, and I... and I..." Winnie sucked in a breath a second before launching himself into Gregory "I'm sorry! Don't be mad! Please don't leave me! I'll do better! I'll... I'll clean up the mess, and I'll... I'll..."

His son's words alone succeeded where multiple terrorists had failed to break him. "Oh, Kiddo," he breathed, carefully pushing Winnie back just enough to cup his cheek with his hand and look at his frosting-encased face. A face he loved more than anything. "I'm not mad at you. I could never be mad at you for something like this. And I'm *never ever* going to leave you, okay? I don't care how many times I have to remind you; that fact is never going to change."

Winnie sniffed, ducking his head as he wiped at his nose. "But...I don't have a gift for you anymore."

Gregory smiled. "I don't need a gift," he said. "I have you. Now...how about we get you cleaned up?" He glanced over at the oven with smoke pouring out of it and it was then the smoke detector finally decided to do its job of annoying people.

Sighing, he quickly shut the oven off and climbed onto the counter to get the smoke detector, and once he had it off, he jumped back down and stepped back toward Winnie. "Like I was saying," Gregory said, flashing Winnie a grin. "Let's clean this place up a bit, then get you cleaned."

Winnie sniffed. "You don't have to help me," he whispered. "I made the mess, and… and it's your birthday."

Snorting, Gregory reached out and ruffled up Winnie's hair. "And miss out on this bonding experience?" he asked, then he glanced at his hand and realized it was covered in frosting. He shrugged and licked it off. "Not bad."

Winnie rolled his eyes. "You're weird."

"'Thanks," Gregory said, flashing him a grin before he clapped his hands together. "All right, let's start by getting the cake out before it decides to take up permanent residence."

Nearly two hours later, the kitchen was clean again, and the only sign of the cake fiasco was the frosting that still clung to Winnie's hair, face, and clothing.

Thankfully, all Gregory had to do was pull the birthday card before he was able to get Winnie to agree to a shower, which was a nice change.

Once they were both cleaned up and had changed into the dorky matching pajamas Gregory's mother had gotten them (which Gregory only kept because they were *really* soft), they made their way down to the living room, and Gregory plopped himself onto the couch and sighed.

"What do you think, Kiddo? Movie and pizza?" he asked, raising an eyebrow at Winnie.

Winnie seemed to hesitate a second before launching himself into Gregory.

"I'm sorry for ruining the cake. This... this is your first birthday without Mom here, and I... I wanted to make it special," Winnie whispered, burying his face against Gregory's chest as he clung to his shirt. "Everyone suggested I draw something, but I hate drawing, and it always looks stupid. I just wanted to make you something good you'd like. Instead I just ruined your birthday."

Sighing, Gregory wrapped his arms around his son's small frame and kissed the top of his curly head. "You didn't ruin anything," he whispered, running his hand through Winnie's still-damp hair. "Having you here is all I could ask for, because you mean everything to me, Kiddo. You're my world, Winnie. And getting to spend the afternoon with you was the best gift you could give me," he said before snorting. "Though I can think of a few more fun things we could have done together."

Winnie groaned, but Gregory could tell by the way his body had relaxed that he knew Gregory meant it. "Love you, Daddy," Winnie whispered, curling up against Gregory's side.

Gregory's throat tightened before he kissed Winnie on the forehead. "And that's the best gift you could ever give me." He cleared his throat and reached for the remote. "So, you want to help me pick the movie, or am I going to have to pick something you'll just *love?* Like one of those kids' shows that make your brain feel numb afterward?"

Moaning, Winnie turned and buried his face against Gregory's side. "Never mind, I take it back. I no longer love you."

Snorting, Gregory ruffled up Winnie's hair before turning his attention back to the TV. "*Fine.* I'll pick something out, you drama queen," he said, wrapping his arm around Winnie and tugging him to his side as he flipped through the channels.

It was far from the most exciting birthday he'd ever had, but he wouldn't trade an evening with his *everything* for anything.

I Wish

"MAYBE HE'S RIGHT. Maybe I *am* a worthless wretch." Thirteen-year-old Mica Connely sighed and surveyed the tired face staring back at him in the dirty reflection of the mirror. Mud-brown eyes, complete with matching dark shadows under them. Short brown hair, barely more than a buzz cut. A few pimples that he chose to ignore. And that reddish-brown birthmark that looked like a wine stain splotched under his left eye, the one that caused him so much teasing at school and made his life even more miserable.

Sighing again, Mica closed his eyes, wondering what in the world he should—*could*—do. But everything was out of his control, just as it had always been. Back when Mom was still with them, life had been different. Lighter; happier.

But when she left, four years ago, everything changed. Mica shook his head wryly. It seemed as if "everything" might be a pretty fitting motto for his life. Everything, yet nothing.

The sound of the front door opening with its signature long, witch-like creak made him jump, and he hurried out of the bathroom with quiet, practiced steps. And just as he had so many times before, he slipped out the back door, swinging his backpack over his shoulders as he went, his father none the wiser.

Everything is *different now, huh?* he thought, scaling the tall wooden fence and landing lightly on the other side. But like always, there was nothing he could do about it.

He headed into the cool shelter of the woods, the one place in which everything had always been the same, the one place his dad had never touched and ruined.

The sound of sirens jolted Mica from the adventures of the merry outlaws of Sherwood Forest. He jumped off the rock he'd been sitting on, his senses on high alert. The sirens didn't stop or fade, and worry pricked its way into his gut. Leaving his book abandoned on the rock, he jumped lightly over the small trickle of a creek and darted through the trees. Peeking through a hole in the fence, he saw flashes of bright red and blue lights, and the frenzied barking of the dogs was unmistakable.

The fear that had been growing steadily intensified, and before he was even aware of what he was doing, Mica was on the other side of the fence and running toward the house. But when he rounded the corner, he skidded to an abrupt stop.

Two uniformed officers were standing at his front door, talking to Mica's father. From where Mica stood, he could hear his dad wasn't happy. He wasn't outright yelling at the cops, but he certainly wasn't being polite, either.

Mica squeezed his eyes shut for an instant, hoping

that when he opened them again, the officers would be gone. Then his father spotted him. "You, boy! Over here!"

The cops turned as Mica slowly trudged towards them, his heart pounding. *Stupid!* he scolded himself. Why'd he let them see him?

"You tell them I ain't been fighting no dogs," Keven Connely growled when Mica had made his way over and was standing at the bottom of the sagging porch.

Mica's heart sank even further as he struggled to find words that wouldn't make this even worse. *This is it, isn't it?*

"Huh, boy? You mute or somethin'?" his father prodded.

"I... I, uh..." Mica started, but the taller cop shook his head.

"You don't need to answer that, son."

"You don't tell *my* son what to do!" Keven's eyes flashed as red crept up his neck and into his face.

"If you haven't got any dogs," the shorter officer said, "then surely you don't have a problem with us checking out the place?"

"You ain't got no warrant! Get off my property!"

"As a matter of fact," she said, "we do." She held up an official-looking piece of paper, and Keven squinted at it.

"You won't find nothing! I don't have no fighting dogs! Leave me alone! I ain't hurt anyone!" But his voice sounded strained, and maybe for the first time in Mica's life, he saw fear on his father's face.

The last time Mica saw his father, Keven had been handcuffed and forced into a police car: destination, jail. The look of pure anger and resentment on the burly man's face sent shivers down Mica's spine.

The taller officer stood next to him, silent, as they watched the car turn and disappear out of view behind the forest foliage. Fighting back the panic that threatened to overwhelm him, Mica turned to the officer. "What's gonna happen now?"

"You'll be in foster care until we can find a relative for you to live with. Your dad could face a sentence of up to five years—dog fighting is no light charge around here, son. I'm just sorry that kids like you are caught up in it."

Mica nodded, biting his lip. *Up to five years?* He'd be eighteen then, an adult. As if seeing the fear and doubt on Mica's face, the officer gave him a reassuring smile.

"It'll be okay. Don't you worry."

But as Mica watched more officers and humane society workers loading the dogs into their vans through his bedroom window as he packed his meager belongings, he couldn't help but worry.

His life was shattering once again, and there was nothing he could do except give the tall officer a brave smile as he slid into the passenger seat of a police car, headed for an unknown future.

The next few days were a blur of new surroundings, new faces, and new everything to Mica. He spent less than a week with a nice lady named Mrs. Goldsmith, an emergency foster parent. Then he was told that they had located an uncle who had agreed to take him in, and everything changed yet again.

Nervousness churned in Mica's gut as he scanned the airport crowds for a man he had barely even known existed, much less ever expected to be suddenly thrust into the care of. He could only imagine how his uncle felt, having a kid to look after now. Especially one as worthless as himself.

At least Lisa, Mica's social worker, seemed to know whom it was they were waiting for, and when a tall, tanned man wearing a cowboy hat came into view, she walked toward him with purposeful strides, leaving Mica no choice but to follow her like a lost puppy. He swallowed hard, trying to ignore the knot tightening painfully in his middle, wishing that he could hide the birthmark that marred his face, telling all the world how he didn't belong.

"Randall Greene, I presume?" Lisa asked, shaking the man's hand.

"That'd be me. And this is Mica?" the man said, studying the boy in front of him with scrutinizing eyes.

Mica nodded, shifting uncomfortably, and Lisa glanced at her watch.

"I really am sorry, but I've got to be going... Are you two fine here?"

No, Mica thought, *how could I be?* But he just nodded again. Everything was so very out of control, and he hated that he was just as helpless as a newborn pup.

Then it was just Mica and his uncle—a complete stranger. Mica forced himself to pick his gaze up from the man's muddy boots and meet his light brown eyes—showing weakness was something he'd learned never led to anything good, and who knew what this new guardian of his would do?

"It's nice to meet you, Mica," the man said in a distinctive Texas twang, "although I'm sorry it's got to be under such unfortunate circumstances."

Mica swallowed hard. "Same to you, sir."

"You wouldn't remember me, would you? You were just a toddlin' thing when we last met," Uncle Randall said. "Helena brought you down to Texas for Christmas. She and Keven were so proud of you." He smiled faintly, then shook his head. "A shame, but there's no going back to the old days. Those all the bags you have?" He nodded at Mica's large duffle bag and backpack.

Mica nodded, hoping that it wasn't too much. "Yessir."

"Alrighty, then. There's about an hour before the plane leaves. You hungry?"

Mica shook his head, even though his stomach protested. He'd been too nervous to eat breakfast, but the last thing he wanted to do was inconvenience his uncle even more.

At the terminal, waiting for the flight, Mica sat tensely on a hard plastic chair, his eyes darting all about, taking in the commotion of the airport. He gripped the armrest tightly and glanced at his uncle; luckily, the man didn't seem to notice Mica's unease. Instead, he was frowning at the screen of his cell phone.

Mica bit the inside of his cheek, worry seeping into his mind. What was wrong? Had something happened and Uncle Randall couldn't take him after all? Where would he go?

"Mica." The firm, soft voice made the boy snap his head up. "There's a bit of a problem down in Texas. A dog was hit by a car—hurt pretty bad, but she'll be okay—and they want me to take her 'til she's well enough to go to the shelter." He gave a boyish grin. "They always try to hook me up with the injured dogs. I think they hope I'll fall in love with one of them someday and wanna keep 'em."

34

Mica nodded slowly, his mind racing to figure out what he was saying. Was his uncle going to leave him, not wanting to take care of both a good-for-nothing boy and an injured dog?

"I s'pose I'll take her in. I'm a bit of a softie—" He winked at Mica as if sharing a secret. "But I wanted to make sure you're fine with it."

Mica was taken aback by being asked, but he was careful not to let it show. "Yessir, that's fine." He wasn't at all sure it was fine, but what could he say? He just hoped that this dog, whatever it was, was nothing like his father's pit bulls.

Uncle Randall gave a wide grin and turned back to his phone, his fingers flying across the screen.

As the plane taxied and bumped its way along the landing strip, Mica stared out the window at the blur of desert landscape and open blue sky. Would he like it here? Would it be better than before? Would his uncle beat him, yell at him, making sure Mica knew just how miserable and despicable he was?

"Home, sweet home," Uncle Randall said with a warm smile, breaking Mica out of his thoughts. "I hope you like it here."

A short time later, they were walking out the airport doors into the bright Texas sunlight, luggage in tow. The dry, hot heat that beat down was a sharp contrast to Kentucky's humid climate. *It's so...different,* Mica thought, resisting the urge to bite his already chewed-up lip.

"Here's our ride," Uncle Randall said when they

reached a mud-splatted, cherry-red pickup truck. He tossed Mica's bags in the bed, gestured to Mica to take the passenger seat, and hopped in.

The ride to Uncle Randall's house was quiet, and almost before Mica knew it, they had pulled up at a small house in a nice-looking neighborhood.

Mica's room was a converted guest room, decorated with all kinds of wooden knickknacks. A wooden loft bed had a small desk underneath, and a large window dappled light onto the beige rug. It was much cooler than his old room back home, but even with his clothes and few possessions unpacked, it still wasn't *his*. Even his dog-eared copy of *Robin Hood*, placed carefully on the bedside table, didn't make it feel like home. Not that he was complaining, of course, but everything about this place was different than what he was used to. Mica tried to not let it bother him, not let it hurt...but it hurt. But there was nothing he could do except grin and bear it as his father had taught him.

"You all settled in?" Uncle Randall asked, poking his head in the open doorway. "Hey, looks pretty good in here."

Mica bit back a shy smile and looked down.

"I was gonna ask you if you wanted to come to pick up the dog. It's been a long day, and I'm sure you're tired, so if you wanna stay here that's all right, too," his uncle continued. "It's up to you."

Mica shook his head. He didn't want to be alone in this stranger's house, and he needed to know the lay of the land around this place, anyway. "I'll come."

The hot Texas sun shone brightly as Mica stepped out

of the truck and jumped down to the black tarmac parking lot of the veterinary clinic. He followed his uncle inside, where a receptionist greeted them cheerfully.

"Ah, Officer Randall! Good to see you! And this must be Mica. Welcome to our humble little town! We're so glad to have you! The dog's in the back. Go on in; Shay'll be there. He'll tell you everything you need to know. Thanks so much for agreeing to take her in. You don't know how much we appreciate this." She paused to catch her breath, shot them a toothpaste-commercial-worthy smile, and gestured towards a nearby door.

"Thanks, Mell," Uncle Randall said and headed over, Mica following meekly behind, still trying to process the lady's words. Of course, he'd been told his uncle was an officer, but somehow, he hadn't quite grasped that fact before now. And how did this Mell lady know about him?

His thoughts were cut short as his uncle pushed open the door and a short, dark-skinned man in a white lab coat greeted them.

"Over here, Randall," the man said immediately, leading the way through what looked like a small hospital. He stopped at a kennel and nodded to the medium-sized dog laying inside. "We're not sure about the breed—some sort of Shetland mix, unless I miss my mark. She wasn't hit too hard, but she fractured her leg. She doesn't have a collar or a microchip, so we're thinking she's a stray. Pretty standoffish, too, which hints at possible abuse and poor socialization."

Uncle Randall nodded. "Sounds like I got myself a troublesome one, huh?"

The man laughed. "Don't you always? Hey, who's this little guy?" he asked, as if only then noticing Mica hovering behind them.

"My nephew, Mica. I told you he was coming to live

with me. Mica, this is Dr. Shay. He's the vet here."

"Howdy, Mica. Nice to have another kid around the place. You're welcome to lend a hand around here anytime." Dr. Shay winked and went on to explain how to care for the dog.

Mica crouched down, keeping his distance even with the wire door that separated them, and ran his eyes over her. She watched him warily with intelligent brown eyes but made no move to either greet or shy away from him. Her brownish-orange and black fur was thick, and she had snowy white paws and a white blaze on her pointed muzzle. All in all, she greatly resembled a tri-colored fox, and she was the complete opposite of the pit bulls that Mica knew so well.

"You're pretty, girl," he muttered softly. *I wonder what your story is.*

"She needs a name," Uncle Randall said that evening after he'd gotten the dog situated in a kennel in the den.

Mica looked at him, a little grin twitching at the corners of his mouth.

"Ah? You have an idea?" Uncle Randall asked.

"Robin," Mica said softly. "Like Robin Hood, 'cause she looks like a fox." It was almost the most he'd said since he'd met his uncle—it felt like weeks ago, not just hours.

Uncle Randall nodded slowly, a grin spreading across his face. "Robin. I like it. How 'bout it, girl?" he asked, turning towards the dog, who only looked at him the same, aloof way. He shrugged. "Suit yourself, dog. You're Robin now, whether you like it or not. Although—" He lowered his voice conspiringly— "I'd suggest that you like it, because

Mica's gonna be taking care of you."

I will? Mica's surprised gaze snapped up to meet his uncle's.

"Yep," Uncle Randall said, as if reading Mica's thoughts. "She's all yours—if you want, anyway. I figured you'd be bored without school or anything, and I'll be busy with work."

Mica swallowed. "Uh... sure." But why would his uncle really trust him to take care of her? And Mica wasn't so sure he trusted the dog, either. Not after the pit bulls.

His mind flashed back menacing growls and hate-filled eyes, dogs circling and lunging, tearing into each other while the men cheered them on. He clenched his jaw, focusing on the gray strands of the carpet at his feet.

"But don't get too attached, okay?" Uncle Randall warned. "We're only fostering her, after all. She may still have owners looking for her."

Mica nodded. He understood, but as he watched Robin staring at them with her unwavering gaze, he couldn't help but wish that things were different. That she could be the dog he'd always longed for, one that didn't have to fight. A pet that he would take for walks, tell his secrets to, love and be loved by.

Dream on, kid, Mica told himself, tearing his gaze away from the dog. "I... I think I'll go to bed now, if that's okay."

Uncle Randall nodded and offered him a warm smile. "'Night, Mica."

Mica left the room but hesitated in the doorway. His uncle was staring at the wall, an expression on his face that Mica had never seen before. Something akin to concern and worry mixed with responsibility and maybe a bit of overwhelmedness... but Mica shook his head and softly padded away. He wasn't any good at reading people, anyway, and even if Uncle Randall seemed nice now, who knew what he was really like?

It was dark when the sound of barking woke Mica up with a jolt. He stared into the darkness, eyes wide, waiting for the sound of his dad cursing and slamming the door to go out and shut the dogs up. The neighbors always complained when they were loud, especially at night.

But the barking continued, and Mica realized that it was different than the bulls—sharper, higher-pitched. His half-asleep mind took a few seconds to process that, and then he sat bolt upright. He was in Texas now, at his uncle's house—and the barking dog was Robin. Mica's responsibility.

Oh, no. Mica pushed the covers away and practically jumped down from the loft bed. He ran downstairs to the den, where Robin was standing up in her crate and raising a din loud enough to wake the dead.

"Robin, quiet!" Mica soothed, slowly walking closer to the riled dog. His heart pounded, his one mission to get her quiet before his uncle woke up—if he hadn't already. "Robin, it's okay, girl. Shush!"

She stared at him but didn't stop barking.

"What's wrong, girl?" Mica made his voice as calm as possible, even though he felt anything but. "Quiet, girl, c'mon, will you?"

Her eyes followed him warily, watching his every move. He walked slowly across the room and sat down near the crate. "It's okay, girl," he crooned softly. "You've gotta be quiet, okay? People like to sleep, you know, like, the whole night long and not be interrupted by a crazy dog." He kept his voice low and soothing, hoping his words would calm her. And gradually, her barking fit slowed. "Yeah, good girl, Robin. That's it. Nice and easy. See, you're okay, aren't you, girl? You're pretty even when you're barking up a storm, you know that? The dogs at my old place"—for it was old now, wasn't it?—"were pretty too, but they got beat up and stuff. They weren't pets, of course, but... Well, I bet you'd make a real good house dog if you'd just settle down and trust us."

Robin gave a low whine, and Mica laughed softly. "Yeah, sure, easy, huh? I wonder what your life was like. Was it hard? Did you get beaten? Did people yell at you? Were you alone, too? Well, girl, you're safe here. No one's going to hurt you, okay?"

Robin yawed and whined again. She was lying down now, her casted leg stretched out straight.

"See, girl, you're okay. Can I go back to bed now?" But when he stood up, Robin struggled to her feet and gave a sharp bark, staring at him as if willing him to stay.

"Nah, girl, I really can't. If I'm out of bed when Uncle Randall comes down..." He didn't finish his sentence, slowly backing away.

Robin barked again, louder this time. Mica winced and bit his lip. "Really, girl?"

She gave a little whine, gazing at him with deep mocha eyes that looked so...lonely. Maybe he was reading into things too much, but he sighed and stepped back to the dog. "You really want me, girl? No one wants me. Why would you?"

Still as a statue, she watched him. He kneeled in front of the crate, wondering what she'd do. No way she'd go from not trusting anything to letting him get that close—but she did. He knew how to read a dog, and she was saying that she was okay with him there, but why? What'd he do?

Taking a deep breath, he slowly unlatched the door, carefully watching the dog inside. She was totally at ease.

"Is that okay, girl? Is this what you want?" He started to slowly pull open the wire door. "Okay, Robin? You're not gonna bite, are you?"

Her eyes said no, she wouldn't hurt him...

"But why would I trust you?" Mica froze, panic shooting through him. "Why'd I trust you? You're a stranger dog, a perfect stranger, and I got bit by the dogs that'd known me since they were born. Why would I trust *you*, dog? Huh?" Mica's voice shook, and his hand dropped to his knee. "What am I *doing*, Robin?" he asked desperately. "Huh, girl?" His voice was dangerously close to breaking. He'd been able to keep himself together all that day, and the days before, but now, under the cover of darkness, the tears came, trailing down his face, dripping down, down, down. Worn out from trying to keep strong, trying to keep everything from completely falling apart, Mica sobbed in the quiet of the darkened house.

Then something warm and wet was licking his hand, and he looked up through bleary, tear-filled eyes to see that Robin had limped forward and pushed the door open just enough to reach him.

Somehow, this dog that was so wary just an hour before had decided to trust him. "Why, dog?" Mica whispered, his voice choked. Robin whined softly, looking into his face, and he scooted back and let the dog push open the door and hop out on three legs. She whimpered again and licked his face, wiping away the salty tears that streamed faster than ever, neither of them noticing the man standing in the doorway, watching them tenderly through tears of his own.

When the sun rose over the early-morning haze of the mountains, the desert of shimmering sand, and the sage bushes, shining in through the large window in the den, it illuminated the sleeping form of a boy and his dog, peaceful and serene.

The sound of footsteps jerked Mica awake, and he sat up with a start, blinking away the grogginess in his eyes. Uncle Randall stood in the doorway, watching him.

With a gulp, Mica scrambled to his feet, Robin copying him. "I'm sorry—I can explain!" Mica's words burst out in a rush, his eyes wide, his heart pounding like a frightened bird's. "She was barking, and I didn't want to wake you, and she wanted to go out of the crate—honest!"

At the distraught sound of the boy's voice, Robin whimpered softly and pressed herself into his slightly trembling legs. This served to calm Mica down, but barely.

"Mica," Uncle Randall started, crossing the room to stand in front of the boy. Mica cringed and barely restrained the urge to bite his lip. He put up his hands to shield his face and braced himself for the blow he knew he deserved. But none came. In surprise, Mica slowly lowered his hands and looked up to see his uncle regarding him with kindness and pity in his brown eyes.

"I'm not going to hit you, Mica," he said softly. "Never. No matter what happened to you before—you're safe here, okay?"

Mica nodded hesitantly, not understanding. Safe? Where was he ever "safe"? For years, the only person he could rely on was himself. The people who were supposed to protect him had hurt him in a way no one else could have, a way that made him lose his trust in the kindness of humanity.

And his uncle was a police officer, someone Mica's father had told him never to trust. The same people who had taken his father away to jail. Yet Uncle Randall, in the short time Mica had known him, had proven himself more trustworthy than Kevin ever had.

Biting his lip without realizing it, Mica studied his uncle, who had kneeled, patiently waiting for Robin. At first, the dog stood by Mica, then started hesitantly forward, limping on her three good legs. She pressed her nose into Uncle Randall's outstretched hand and let him stroke her head, her plume of a tail wagging, slowly picking up speed.

Before his eyes, Mica watched the dog begin to trust. If she could, then so could he…right?

So, taking a deep breath, Mica vowed that he would learn to trust again. Somehow. But even if it took a while—even if it was hard—he wanted to be able to rely on others, to not always be questioning their motives. He wanted to be free.

And at that moment, everything seemed like maybe, just maybe, it would be okay. Not perfect, but okay.

One Year Later

"Fetch, girl!" Mica called, hurling the frisbee with all his might. Robin flew after it; with a graceful leap, she nabbed the yellow disc out of the air. She ran back to her boy and dropped the frisbee by his feet. He picked it up and was about to throw it again when Uncle Randall appeared on the back porch.

"Mica! Dinner!"

"We'll come out later, okay, girl?" Mica promised, and

Robin grinned up at him, panting slightly. "You sure run a whole lot better than you did with that awful cast on, huh?" The memory of his dog lumbering awkwardly after a tennis ball made him laugh. But now, her broken leg was a thing of the past.

"Race you to the house!" Mica shouted suddenly, taking off. But Robin had winged feet and quietly outdistanced him, leaving the boy in her dust. She leaped up the three steps in one bound and skipped to a stop beside Uncle Randall, who laughed and bent down to scratch behind her butterfly ears.

Things sure have changed, Mica thought as he sat at the dinner table, watching his uncle say grace. When he had arrived last year, he'd been so frightened and out-of-place; now he almost felt as if he'd lived in Texas all his life. Uncle Randall had proven himself different from Mica's parents time and time again. And Robin was Mica's dog. Uncle Randall had given her to him not long after he'd first come to stay. They said a dog was a boy's best friend, and even though the pit bulls hadn't exactly been such, Robin was everything Mica had dreamed of, and more.

Yes, Mica thought. *Everything is different...and I wouldn't change it for the world.*

THE END

EVERYTHING
BY SANDRALENA HANLEY

Stepping Past Fear

AMY TWITCHED THE curtain beside the front door, watching until the Amazon truck drove away. Only when she was sure the driver could not see her in his mirror did she open the door. She quickly pulled the box with the smiling arrow inside.

Amazon was a lifesaver, literally. Otherwise Amy would need to leave the house to buy what she wanted. And Amy hadn't left the house in ten years.

Everything scared Amy: semi-trucks, cars, traffic, crowds, dogs, and wildlife—everything outside her house, her oasis. All of it was unsafe. That is what she had decided when she was eighteen and in a "road rage" traffic accident. The physical scars had healed but not the psychological ones.

The phone rang. Amy glanced at it. She almost declined to answer. Her mother called every week to check in on her. It always ended the same way, with an argument about Amy's choice of life. She sighed. Might as well get it over with since her mom would keep ringing every ten minutes until she answered. Obviously, she was home.

Putting the package down, she sat on the edge of an ancient recliner and answered.

"Hello, Mom." She tried to sound upbeat, but her neck muscles tightened.

"I hope I'm not interrupting your work."

"No. I just got the mail. I ordered new sandals." She regretted it the moment she said it. She should have discussed the weather, or her latest library book.

She heard her mother sigh. "Honey, if you had asked, I would've taken you shopping." Disappointment tinged her voice. "In fact, we can still go." Persuasion escalated. "Browse the stores in the mall. Buy you some new clothes. Have a cup of coffee. Just like old times." Her mother had that tone to her voice. Hopeful, yet resigned.

"I'm afraid not. I can get everything I need online." Amy clenched the phone and waited for the outburst she knew was coming.

Her mother's voice rose. "You *need* to get out of the house. Mingle with real people." She paused, then spoke softly. "Honey, you survived the totaling of your car. I know it wasn't easy."

Easy? It was weeks in the hospital and months of physical therapy. She healed, but she would never be the same.

And the look of fury the truck driver had sent her for merely passing him had shattered her trust in the basic goodness of humans. As he sideswiped her car, his face was a mixture of hate and glee as he forced her into the traffic pole. The episode haunted her dreams for years. Amy broke out in a sweat at the memory.

"It's been ten years, Amy. It is about time you come out of your shell and live!" Her mom's exasperation echoed across the line. "Please, honey. God's got this. You just have to trust Him."

"I'll think about it." It was a lie, but what was she supposed to say? "I've got to go. Love you." She hung up, guilt settling in the pit of her stomach. She hated lying.

Amy's relationship with God was nonexistent. She knew she should pray. Maybe then she would heal. Saying "trust God" and actually doing it were very different. Why had He let her be injured in the first place?

Why leave the house? Amy had everything she needed.

She glanced around the familiar room as she carried her package to the kitchen. She had moved in with her grandmother to recuperate. The bookcases were stuffed with her favorite reads, the cuckoo clock was always behind time with its little Swiss girl and boy dancing in and out the doors, and the wooden swan held open the bathroom door that would otherwise swing shut. The smell of vanilla and lemon polish reminded her of her grandmother, now dead.

Grandmother had understood. That's why she left Amy the house. She told Amy that when she was good and ready, Amy would be brave enough to leave.

The time just wasn't yet. But the longer she waited to leave the safety of the old-fashioned house, the harder it became.

Amy dumped the package on the kitchen counter and dug through the junk drawer for a pair of scissors. Slicing through the tape, she pulled out the brown sandals she had ordered. She slipped them on. They fit perfectly. Because, of course, she always bought the same brand of shoes. That way there were no surprises. She threw last year's model with the cracked soles in the garbage.

She admired her new sandals as she walked over to her computer station. The only other person who would see them was her best friend Lacy.

Lacy worked at the library. She was due to come over this afternoon for her weekly book drop off. Amy chose what she wanted to read from the library's online catalog and Lacy pulled them off the shelf and hand-delivered them. It wasn't exactly library policy, but they had done it for so many years that the staff didn't complain.

As if her friend knew Amy was thinking about her, a text from her dinged.

Hey, girl.

Hey.

I met this cute guy at the coffee shop. It turns out we went to Central High together, three grades apart. We're going to hang out together this weekend. Did you try out that new dating app I shared?

At least Lacy didn't nag her to go outside. Her angle was trying to convince Amy into online dating.

No. What is the use? Most guys eventually want to meet in person.

A pause. Amy tapped her foot, waiting for Lacy to launch into why it could still work.

I'll drop off the books at 5.

Thanks. See you then.

Either her friend was busy with a library patron, or she couldn't think of a good argument.

Pushing aside her empty mug from the morning, Amy sat at her computer. She wiggled the mouse until the screen came on. Census data from 1950 filled the screen. Her notebook lay beside the mouse. Amy made a modest living as a genealogist for hire. Her first client had been the head of the local DAR chapter. Because Amy had broken through the woman's brick wall and proved her ancestors sailed aboard the Mayflower, Amy was allowed to check out books from the DAR library on special loan.

Those books were neatly stacked for return since she had fulfilled her last contract. She had solved the mystery of the two wives of Samuel Brayton, proving Polly and Abigail were sisters. Although she could not understand how a girl named Mary could have the nickname Polly. *Polly put the kettle on. Suki took it off again.* The old rhyme ran through her head. She had no idea what it meant.

But somehow, today she wasn't able to get down to work. Maybe it was the soft breeze floating through the chintz curtains. She wandered over to the kitchen window. The summer breeze was warm, bringing the tantalizing smell of wisteria.

A squirrel hung upside down on the feeder, snatching birdseed in his little hands and stuffing his cheeks. Amy smiled at his antics. But the feeder was low. It would be late this afternoon before Lacy could fill it. Amy frowned.

She moved over to her well-stocked pantry. Between Door Dash and Walmart deliveries, she had everything she could want. Pushing aside the Boom Chicka Pop popcorn, she located a large bag of peanuts. It had appealed to her the day she bought it, but she really wasn't a peanut fan.

Taking it over to the back door, she opened the door and stood just inside the doorway. The squirrel stopped what he was doing and eyed her. She tore open the top of the bag and stepping to the edge of the doorsill, she threw some peanuts his way.

He swung for an undecided moment, then scrambled down and hopped toward the new treat. He stuffed his cheeks full, then ran away to a nearby stump. Pulling out a peanut, he examined it, then opened it and ate.

Somewhere nearby, a lawn mower roared into life, and soon Amy smelled new cut grass.

The squirrel finished his treat. Instead of running

away, he moved closer and closer. When he was only five feet away, he rose on his back paws and seemed to beg. Amy felt as if he were asking her to give him a peanut directly.

Keeping her eye on him, she moved closer, one step at a time. She bent down and stretched her arm out with a nut. He snatched it from her hand, hopped a few feet away, and ate it leisurely. Done, he ran up her maple tree and waved his tail at her.

"I trained him to eat out of my hand."

Amy spun around and found a little girl of about seven standing on the edge of her cement pad.

"I didn't mean to scare you." The girl had blond pigtails and freckles across her nose. She wore a t-shirt with a sparkly unicorn on it and bright pink shorts. "My name is Jasmyn. What's yours?'

"Amy."

"I love mister squirrel, although my mom is always trying to find a way to get rid of him. She says he eats all the bird food." She swung her bookbag back and forth. "That's silly. Everyone in the neighborhood has a bird feeder. No one has a squirrel feeder. I think it's unfair. Have you been sick?"

Amy blinked at the rapid change in conversation. "Um, no, not really."

"It's just that I've never seen you before. And your skin is pale, like when Anne was ill and stayed inside all summer. I couldn't imagine staying inside all the time. No hopscotch." She dropped her bookbag and hopped to make her point. "No scooter, no chalk drawings, or playing on the swingset." She picked up a peanut Amy had dropped and threw it toward the maple tree. "Do you have any children?"

Again, the question caught Amy off guard. "No, I'm not married." And she wasn't likely to be if she couldn't move on with her life.

"Then maybe you could be my friend. Would you let me climb your tree?" Without waiting, Jasmyn ran over and pulled herself up into Amy's maple tree. The squirrel chittered and ran up higher.

Jasmyn sat on the lowest branch, swinging her legs. "We don't have a tree to climb in my yard." She pointed over the fence to the next yard. The top of a swingset showed over the wall, as well as several poplar trees.

"Jasmyn!"

"That's my mom. I'd better go." She jumped out of the tree and stuck out her hand. "Nice meeting you." She grabbed her bookbag and started to skip away, then turned around. "I'll have to tell the other kids on the block that they were wrong about you."

"Why? What do they say about me?"

"That you are a spooky lady. That something must be wrong with you because you never leave your house. But you did come out today." She waved her hand and ran off.

Amy stood stock still. She had forgotten that she stood outside, lured by the squirrel.

The children on the street were afraid of her? She was one of those scary people that children have nightmares about?

And here she was just trying to avoid all the scary things in life.

Everything.

She avoided everything.

And yet, what was so terrifying about standing outside in the sunshine? She lifted up her face. The warm sun felt so good, like her grandmother's embrace.

And why was talking to a stranger so scary? Jasmyn had showed her how it easily it could be done.

Amy deliberately walked over to her grandmother's

painted iron deck chair and sat down. She could glimpse the street through the gaps in the fence. Children were walking home from school. A jet passed overhead. The mower shut down.

Have mercy on me, O God, have mercy on me. For my soul trusteth in Thee. And in the shadow of Thy wings will I hope.

Her grandmother's favorite verse from the Book of Psalms popped into her mind.

She decided she would eat her lunch outside. Somehow, looking at it from the outside, the house seemed small and cramped.

Wait till Lacy came over today.

EVERYTHING
BY E.N. LEONARD

The Everything and the Infinite

I WATCH THE world pass by;
I know You've seen it all.
You've seen the kingdoms rise,
And now I watch them fall.
I saw the green buds grow
Into aspen leaves in awe;
I saw them turn to gold,
And now I watch them fall.
O Lord of everything,
The earth beneath Your feet,
I draw so near to You,
O Lord, I'm on my knees.
I try to distill Love,
The wonder of Your all,
As well as my grieving
To see earth fade and fall.
You lead out the stars,
So, Lord, I sing in awe,

And You tell me to sing
Though now I watch them fall.
O Lord of everything,
Your mercy never ends.
Can't have new beginning
Without the old one's end.
Everything that begins
Will one day fade and fall,
Yet from the ashes rise
Your glories, bringing awe.
You burn the chaff away;
Lord, You renew us all.
Then we praise in Your day
And worship in Your hall.
O Lord of everything,
Holy is Your great Name!
I praise the One who makes,
Gives, takes, and renews all!

EVERYTHING
BY BETHANY WILLCOCK

EVERYTHING COMES IN circles.

Sherlock Holmes had said that. I humphed as I flung the filthy old burlap sack I'd been examining back onto the heap of rubbish in the corner. It brushed a few cobwebs, sending a shower of old dust raining down on both me and the pile. I sneezed for what must have been the ten millionth time.

"That is all fine and well, Mr. Holmes," I muttered grumpily, lifting the hem of my dark skirt off the floor and stalking away from the corner. "But how does that help us solve anything, pray?"

"Cathryn Lloyd!" Helene's urgent hiss floated across the dirty floorboards of the overstuffed attic. I spun round and she gestured at me desperately. "Cathryn, for pity's sake, be silent! Miss Hurst will hear us and come to investigate if you do not stop stomping around like this!"

I rolled my eyes at my twin. Miss Hurst was the least of our problems right now.

"This is no good." I stepped gingerly over to Helene, taking care not to stomp. "We are getting nowhere. There must be an easier way."

"What? You know perfectly well that Uncle said we would find something important in the attic. How are we to do that unless we hunt for whatever it is?"

"I know." I plonked myself down onto a nearby trunk and tried to ignore the clouds of dust that puffed out under me as I did so. I gazed about us in despair. It was like searching for the proverbial needle, only in that case they at least knew it was a needle they were supposed to be searching for. Unfortunately in ours, Uncle hadn't been so specific.

"Well?" I looked helplessly over at my twin, who with a slight sigh also gave up and dropped wearily onto a broken piano stool. "What exactly did Uncle say again? As in, what were his actual words? There must be a clue in them, surely."

"One would think," murmured Helene, carefully rearranging her long black skirt. I noticed with some alarm that her face was even more pale and drawn than usual. She'd never been terribly strong or well, even as a child. And ever since Uncle's illness and resulting death she'd seemed even worse. I frowned. Maybe I shouldn't have let her assist my search in this dusty, mouldy attic after all. She was already looking so tired.

"He wasn't very specific, was he," Helene went on, oblivious to my concern. "He seemed to be worried Miss Hurst would come in and overhear him."

"Which she nearly did," I pointed out. "She'd only stepped out the room for a minute to fetch his medicine glass. He hardly managed to say as much as he did before she came back in, more's the pity."

Helene nodded thoughtfully. "What could have been so secret that you'd want to hide it from your own sister?" she wondered.

"Half-sister," I corrected. "Thankfully, or we'd have been related to her too. How grim would that have been!"

"Rather grim," Helene agreed. "She and Uncle were never very close anyway. I wonder why he even asked her to come be his housekeeper for him. Anyway, we're getting off track here. He told us to find something important up here after his funeral, so now we must just put our heads together and think. He obviously had confidence that we could find it even though he didn't get to finish telling us what it was. We just need to narrow our search down, somehow."

"But what *is* it? Right now it could literally be anything, which basically narrows it down to *everything!*" I gazed fitfully around at the dust-covered piles of broken furniture, trunks, boxes, and other assorted discards that were no longer wanted, needed, or used, half-hoping the elusive "something" would suddenly fall from whatever dark and dusty corner it had been lurking in and present itself to me.

It didn't, of course.

"Surely it couldn't be as important as Uncle seemed to imply it was, if it's been left up here to rust for who-knows-how-many years?"

Helene, ever the more logical twin, shook her head thoughtfully, her auburn ringlets catching the thin beam of sunlight that had somehow managed to filter through all the boxes and piles from the tiny skylight window on the far end of the attic. "We are not thinking this through properly. We need to apply ourselves and reason this out as Mr. Holmes would do."

"Before he retired to the countryside to keep bees," I added, rather acidly I confess. The public (and by that I most definitely include my sister and myself) had never quite been able to get over the shockwaves that had rippled through our country when Dr. Watson announced through the papers that Sherlock Holmes had finally retired and given up his adventures along with his old quarters in 221B Baker Street to live out his final years as a stuffy old beekeeper. It was heartrending, to say the least, and most alarming too. The streets and byways of London had never been so safe as when he'd roamed them with Dr. Watson, hot on the trail of a criminal mastermind; nor were the papers so interesting when they ceased to print Dr. Watson's fresh accounts of Mr. Holmes' latest triumph.

"At least his knowledge and deductive methods haven't been entirely lost," Helene remarked, as she tried in vain to force off the layers of dust encrusted onto the cracked glass of an oldf ramed photograph that was so filthy I could hardly make out the subjects, although they appeared to be a mother and infant. "What the papers have been lacking in news of Mr. Holmes they've certainly made up for in accounts of that young protégé of his, what's-his-name, Wood—Wood-something…"

"Vincent Woodthorn. Even his name sounds exciting. I read that after Mr. Holmes decided to retire, he was swamped with letters from young men across the country, asking him to assist them in starting up as detectives themselves. But he wasn't interested in any of them until Inspector Lestrade recommended the adopted son of a friend of his, this Vincent Woodthorn, to him for training. They say Mr. Holmes has trained him in all his methods and deducting skills. Now he's setting out for himself and already has quite a renowned reputation that is growing all the time."

"You seem to know a great deal about the man," remarked Helene absently, having given up on the dirty picture frame and turned her attention to another trunk.

"The circumstances surrounding his rise to fame and prestige fascinate me," I admitted. "Only think! After being an orphan your whole life, living with an adopted family, to then be actually noticed and schooled by the great Mr.

Holmes himself! An honour of which precious few can boast. How I would love to meet him. Judging from the papers he is both honourable and kind. And what a life he must now lead!"

"Never mind his life," muttered Helene, still rummaging in the trunk. "It's his brains we could use round about now! Would that he were here; he'd have solved this in an instant!"

"We're simply not applying ourselves correctly." Now it was my turn to be logical. That and I was tired of boxes and dust. I let my eyes wonder around the attic. "All we know is that we have to find something up here that Uncle left for us to help us in some way." I sighed. "I admit it is not very much to go on, is it."

Helene straightened up from her trunk and pursed her already-drawn lips. "It's a bit like Mr. Holmes always said. 'Pay attention to details. Everything is important.'"

"Actually I don't think Mr. Holmes ever did say that, not quite in those words at any rate! But I take your point. Anything *might* be important, therefore everything *is* important." I glanced back towards the corner with the pile of burlap sacks thoughtfully. "Everything is important. Everything is a circle."

"What?" Helene's startled face appeared 'round a stack of old books that had an ancient spinning-wheel Miss Hurst had thrown out years ago reposing haughtily—albeit somewhat askew—on top.

"Oh nothing." I frowned, trying to remember the exact quote and why it should have suddenly sprung into my head at that moment. "Just thinking out loud. Everything is a circle. No, everything *comes* in circles. Yes, that's the right one. Everything comes in circles. It's a quote of Mr. Holmes' that Uncle used to repeat all the time. Don't you remember?

He said it often. I'm just struggling to remember the whole thing."

"I do, vaguely." Helene paused, gazing meditatively at the dust-coated books. "Something about everything being done again the same as before, or some such."

"Yes. Something like that. I wonder—"

"Girls! Where are you? Get yourselves in here now; I wish to speak with you! This instant!"

Helene and I balked and gazed at each other in horror.

"Miss Hurst! What do we do now?" Helene gasped, turning so pale I feared she really was about to faint. I seized her arm to steady her.

"Quick! Make no sound and she may think we are in the garden and cannot hear. Here—" I pushed my handkerchief into her hand, "Take this and clean the dust off your face. Is mine as bad as yours is?"

Helene nodded, her eyes large and frightened in her thin white face as she feverishly dabbed at it with the lace-edged handkerchief. "Is it coming off?" she gasped in a whisper. "Do I look all right? Here, you have a cobweb in your hair, let me fix that—there. What do we do? She's gone into the garden by the sounds of it."

"Then make haste; we haven't a moment to lose. Come!" I pushed her towards the attic stairs and we paused listening at the top. Miss Hurst's angry calls sounded dimmed; surely she must have gone into the garden? Carefully we tiptoed down the creaking stairs and upon reaching the bottom safe and unapprehended, we allowed ourselves a moment to heave a sigh of relief before fleeing silently back to our rooms, hoping we had enough time to properly wash our faces, rearrange our hair, and get all traces of dirt off our floor-sweeping black dresses before Miss Hurst returned inside.

When we finally did answer her furious shouts, we stepped calmly downstairs trying our best to look composed, although Helene, I noticed worriedly, was still extremely pale. We found Miss Hurst waiting for us at the foot of the staircase, her stern, unpleasant face deeply set in an even more unpleasant scowl.

She glared at us.

"Where have you been?" she demanded. Fortunately she gave us no time to reply but impatiently tore from her skirt pocket a letter, which she flourished triumphantly at us.

"I have received a response from my friend Alice Waters. She's agreed to take you both on as *assistants* in her school for young ladies. There you will teach the younger students and also help around the school doing housework and general chores in order to earn your room and board."

"*What?*" I spluttered, not even caring that I was interrupting her. To say that I was incensed would be an understatement of no small proportions. "Our Uncle is barely three days in his grave and you've already made arrangements to have us shipped off to some or other school as *servants?* Worse than servants, for we are not even to earn wages nor have any say in the matter. You have no authority to do this to us!"

"Well it's that or the poorhouse, so take your pick! It certainly is no matter to me either way." Miss Hurst briskly smoothed down her skirt. "It is no fault of mine that you were born and orphaned after your mother's second marriage. I cannot help what my half-brother chose to do in his life, and I'm certainly not going to inherit the responsibility of looking after the pair of you until you come of age simply because I've inherited this house. Your Uncle left no provision for you, and he made no arrangements regarding your futures. I feel that in securing these positions I have gone above and beyond what little duty is expected of me, considering you are not even my own kin."

I tried to speak but Miss Hurst abruptly silenced me with a wave of her hand and went on.

"With no family, no connections, no money, and no prospects, you two girls will never have any chance of surviving unless you marry well or find a good occupation. And considering that without an inheritance or any form of dowry no young man in his right senses would take either of you, it would appear your only option is to go into service somewhere and make yourselves useful. I have taken the trouble to secure you both respectable positions at a respectable establishment and have quite surpassed my duty on the matter. It is settled, and I will hear no more on the subject. Your train leaves at seven tomorrow morning. See that you are both packed and ready by quarter-past six sharp, I will have the carriage waiting." And she turned with a dismissive wave at us.

"Wait!" I cried, leaping down the last few steps and seizing her arm. Miss Hurst paused and turned back to me with a cold, disdainful glare. I rushed on regardless, lowering my voice slightly, hoping my sister could not hear.

"Please. Miss Hurst. You know Helene is unwell. She's never had a very strong constitution *school.* Any form of exercise exhausts her, and now you honestly expect her to do daily strenuous household work for a whole? It will kill her! You know it will surely kill her!"

Miss Hurst's icy stare remained entirely unmoved. She shrugged off my hand.

"And again, as I said, that really is not the slightest concern of mine. If she wants to manage she will grow a stronger constitution. A little hard work never hurt anyone. I have done my duty; nobody could expect me to do more. Go and pack."

I stared helplessly after her then turned slowly back to Helene who was still clinging to the banister, her eyes large and frightened, looking as though she were about to drop, and I saw she was trembling all over.

"Cathryn. What will we do? I can't; I just simply can't. I'm so sorry; I honestly *can't.*"

"It's all right, of course you can't. She's mad to think you can." I put my arm round her shoulders and tried to hide the tremble of fear in my own voice. "We'll think of a way to get out of this somehow, don't worry. I'm absolutely not going to go slave away for some school mistress just because poor Mama had the misfortune to die when we were children, and Papa long before that. Miss Hurst says that's no fault of hers; well then, nor is it ours. We can't help that we're alone and penniless and there's no reason why we should be punished for it in such a cruel way by someone who holds no authority over us."

Helene sniffed and nodded. "But it will be three years before we're of age. How are we going to manage until then? She's right. We can't marry nor get proper paying employment. But what I don't understand is why Uncle didn't say what was to happen with us? He looked after us so well for all these years since Mama died, and it is just not like him to leave us hanging like this, especially not at the mercy of Miss Hurst! Why, he never even liked her much! I think he only left her the house because he knew she'd take it anyway if he didn't. I don't think he really wanted to."

"I can tell you right now he didn't want to!" I was still seething, and very worried, especially for Helene. I was the only family she had now, and by default the only person who could—and would—look after her. But something she had said was nagging at me.

Helene must have noticed because she suddenly asked what was wrong. I slowly shook my head.

"I'm not sure. Something you said. About Uncle. You are right, it's not like him to leave us unprovided for in this way. You know what." I spun round to face her, sudden excitement surging through me. "I don't think he did. He wouldn't have. It wasn't like him; he cared for us too much."

My twin's eyes widened as the realization dawned on her too. "What he told us! About finding something in the attic! That was it, wasn't it? He *did* leave something to look after us! He just couldn't give it to us, so he tried to tell us where to find it but was interrupted by Miss Hurst coming back! Oh, Cathryn! We have to find it before tomorrow. Whatever it is it will mean we won't have to go away!"

"Yes! Yes, you're right!" I seized her hand eagerly and started running up the stairs. "The attic, quick! We really don't have a single moment to lose now."

Back in the attic we paused for a minute, trying to catch our breaths. I gazed around at all the stacks of boxes and trunks. The answer was here. I could feel it, just beyond my reach. It seemed that if I stretched out a little further, I would find it. It somehow felt closer than before, almost as though I already knew part of it, almost as though....

"Everything." The word slipped out before I realised I'd said it. Helene looked at me, surprised.

"Everything what?"

"Everything comes in circles." I started walking slowly down the length of the attic. "It's part of the clue. We don't need Vincent Woodthorn to solve this after all. We already have everything we need to find it ourselves, in our memory. It's here somewhere. We just need to apply ourselves, as you told me earlier."

Helene started following me down the attic. "Uncle always used to say that the knowledge we'd gained through our love of reading Mr. Holmes' cases would stand us in good stead someday."

I stilled. "He did, didn't he." I stared thoughtfully at the attic wall. "In fact, he said it again only a few days before his illness worsened. I remember being struck by it at the time, and now on reflection, it was almost as though, as though…" My voice trailed off.

"As though he were giving us a clue! A warning, almost, that things were about to change."

"Yes." I'd reached the wall at the end of the room and stopped again before the pile of burlap sacks in the corner.

"*Everything comes in circles. The old wheel turns, and the same spoke comes up.* Then how did it go on?"

Helene's voice came from behind a heap of stacked trunks.

"*It's all been done before, and will be done again.* At least, I think that's right."

I nodded eagerly. "Yes! That's it. The old wheel. The same spoke. Everything done again that's been done before. It's in there; I know it is. Keep thinking!"

"I am!" Helene appeared 'round the heap and stood with her hand resting on the stack of old books again, staring at the dust-covered rafters, deep in thought. My eyes travelled from her up the books, finally settling randomly on the old, broken spinning wheel resting on top.

"That's definitely seen better days," I muttered absently, turning away, but as I did so it suddenly dawned on me with the force of lightning.

"The wheel! The old wheel that turns! It's the wheel!"

I leapt past my startled sister with a shriek and started tearing wildly at the books. "It's too high to reach, help me pull these down!"

"No!" Helene darted to my side. "You pull those down and there'll be such a crash you'll have Miss Hurst up here in no time! Here! You're stronger. Give me a leg up."

Cupping my hands to make her a step, I boosted Helene up onto the books and she lunged for the wheel.

"It's awfully heavy. Here, catch hold!" She pulled the spinning wheel from its dusty perch and jumped down. I barely managed to catch it before it reached the floor, bringing down about seven heavy books with it.

Helene winced and I cast a hurried glance towards the attic trapdoor. But no Miss Hurst was appearing angrily through it. Taking courage, I placed the wheel carefully on the floor and crouched down to examine it.

"It's too thin to have anything hidden inside."

I nodded. "Yes, but there is this under part, the base that it's resting on. It's probably big enough to hide something in. Trouble is, I have no idea how to get it open."

Helene leaned over my shoulder and watched as I struggled with the flat, square wooden base that the wheel and stand were attached to. "There doesn't appear to be any seams in it aside from the one running right below the top, all the way around like a lid."

"Well, that has to be it, surely? Unless we have the wrong wheel?" Helene straightened and started casting about the room for inspiration.

I shook my head. "Wait, the second part, about the same spoke coming round. I wonder…"

I rose and Helene handed me a hair ribbon. After tying it to the top spoke, I slowly turned the wheel in a complete rotation, expecting every moment to hear the lid on the base click open, and only once the spoke with the ribbon had come up again and was once more at the top did I realise that this would be much harder than I'd first thought.

"Well, what are our other options?" Helene said after a slight pause.

"I am baffled. I really thought we had it figured out just then." I knelt back down beside the spinning wheel and began to really study it. "Maybe if we had something thin and strong we could force this base open."

Helene glanced around and grabbed the dirty old photograph she'd found earlier. She removed the back of the frame and handed it to me.

"Here, would this work? It's thin and strongish—oh dear! The photograph fell out."

"Let me." As I bent to retrieve it, something pencilled on the back caught my eye. I squinted at the faded words.

"The light is better here by the window." Helene started to move towards it, but her foot caught the corner of a fallen book and she tripped, caught at the wheel to save herself, grabbed a loose spoke instead which promptly came off, and went sprawling over the wheel, taking it with her. At the same moment a frightful banging sounded at the front door downstairs, accompanied by a man's shout then Miss Hurst's angry voice, also raised.

Jumping at the sudden din from all directions, I dropped the photograph to the floor where the filthy glass shattered into a thousand pieces.

Helene struggled up, still clutching desperately at the spoke. Downstairs Miss Hurst was screaming for us, and the man was still shouting.

"Cathryn, look. They were rolled up inside the spoke."

I took the papers Helene quietly handed me and blinked. Confused, I looked back up at my twin.

"I don't understand. Our birth certificates."

"GIRLS!" screeched Miss Hurst from downstairs.

Helene looked as puzzled as I was. "Mama must have placed them here to keep them safe, and they must be what Uncle sent us to look for, but it doesn't make sense. These will hardly stop us being sent away to work."

"GIRLS! GET IN HERE!"

"No, they won't." I was at an utter loss. Nothing was adding up anymore, and we were out of time. I looked at the shattered glass at my feet and automatically bent down and retrieved the photograph. "We'd better go down." I tilted my head towards the door. "Before *she* comes *up*."

"You go." I saw for the first time that Helene had somehow cut her hand on the glass when she fell. She was dabbing at it with her handkerchief. "I'll be down once I get this blood to stop flowing. Don't be alarmed; it's not deep."

I nodded and headed for the door.

Downstairs was in chaos. Miss Hurst had lost all her genteel façade and was howling like a madwoman at the young man in a blue overcoat standing just inside the doorway. He had the air of a gentleman, albeit a rather exasperated one at present. He caught sight of me on the stairs and abruptly dropped whatever argument he was engaged in with Miss Hurst.

"Are you one of the Lloyd twins?" he demanded. Miss Hurst spun around and made a lunge at me.

"You see? You *see*? There is no resemblance, none at *all*!" She shoved me towards the young gentleman and shook me by the shoulders. "All you say are lies! You are a fraud, sir, trained by a deceitful, manipulating, scheming fra—"

"Enough, madame, I have been listening to your insults for the past five minutes and I will listen no longer. It was she I came to see, not you. Where is your sister?" turning back to me.

"Upstairs. She will be down soon."

"And you are…?"

"Cathryn, sir, and most confused."

He flashed me a sudden grin and was about to speak, but Miss Hurst interrupted.

"Do not listen to him, Cathryn; he speaks nothing but lies, for he is one of the most deceitful men in all England."

The gentlemen spun round and took a step towards her. "If I'm speaking lies, how then do you explain this photograph Cathryn just brought down that matches the one I just showed you out of my own pocket?"

He flourished the photograph and only then I realised I'd dropped it. Miss Hurst glanced at it and visibly blanched.

"Impossible," she gasped, sinking heavily onto the step.

He turned back to me. "Who is that woman in the photograph?"

I blinked in amazement. Now that the dirty glass was gone the features were clear.

"It's… Why, it's…my…my mother," I stammered in bewilderment.

"Quite so." He turned it around and held out the back to me. "And what was her maiden name?"

"Spooner?"

"Good, and now what was her last name before she married your father and became a Lloyd?"

"Why, I don't know," I started, but then my eyes fell

71

again on the faded, pencilled name on the back. I stared, stunned.

"Woo—Woodthorn?"

The man nodded. "Her first husband was Andrew Woodthorn. He died in the war. After a year she got remarried, to your father, James Lloyd."

"B-but, but the *baby*...?" I touched the photograph and he nodded.

"Yes. Before she met your father she fell on very hard times. To prevent her small son from ending up in a poorhouse she placed him in the care of a wealthy family who had no children of their own. They raised him, even after she remarried."

"My *mother*. Had a *SON*? And I never even knew?" I could hardly believe what I was hearing.

"It's true, Cathryn."

We all jumped at Helene's quiet statement. Nobody had noticed she'd arrived.

She handed me a large, heavy old Bible, with ornate lettering and a beautifully carved wooden cover—a family Bible.

"I found this near the spinning-wheel. I think it's what Uncle meant us to find, not the birth certificates after all. The wheel was resting on top of it I think, on that book pile, and it fell down when we moved it. Look."

My eyes followed her finger to the open "Births, Deaths, and Marriages" page at the front and read the name she indicated. Suddenly it was as though everything started falling neatly into place inside my muddled head.

Vincent Woodthorn, born to Andrew and Honoura Woodthorn on this day...

Helene and I raised our eyes to the smiling young man. "Indeed." He grinned at the livid Miss Hurst and produced a namecard. "I am Vincent Woodthorn."

"I still don't understand."

The three of us were in the parlour, catching up on our life stories. I was still somewhat dazed by everything. An hour ago, we were wishing Vincent Woodthorn could assist us in our search. Now he was our brother. It took a little getting used to.

"Why is Miss Hurst in such a flap? She was going to send us away to work anyway; why should she care if we are related to you or not?"

Vincent shrugged. "She hates Mr Holmes, and so, by default, me also. Apparently he had her fiancé, Colonel Moran, hanged for murder years ago, and she's never forgiven him. Anyhow, you won't be sent away now that I've found you! Before he died Uncle wrote and told me everything, begging me to do what I could for my sisters. But I was abroad and only received it yesterday. I rushed over as soon as I did."

"Everything's worked out so well!" Helene smiled. "Will we come live with you, or must you get bigger rooms first?"

"Actually, I happen to know of a very decent little place the three of us could rent, and where you can stay safely when I'm away on a case. Recently vacated and right in the centre of things." Vincent grinned. "Ever heard of 221B Baker Street?"

Sherlock Holmes had been right. I grinned at my brother and sister. Everything indeed comes in circles.

EVERYTHING
BY KATJA H. LABONTÉ

ALL MY LIFE I wondered what that old car was doing there—parked away back in the pasture, rusty and alone, and looking like it had stepped straight out of *mon oncle* Alphonse's magazine on vintage cars. No one ever went near it or talked of it, even though Pépère and my uncles were strictly utilitarian and always badgering Mémère to get rid of some sentimental thing or another. Yet Mémère hated cars and was even more ignorant about them than I was. Growing up on a farm full of men taught a young girl many things.

Somehow it never occurred to me to ask about the old car. I had an indefinable feeling that it was just to be tacitly ignored, and I wasn't the kind to dig up old skeletons. But every time my eye caught sight of that red, battered, yet still somehow proud old heap, I wondered again.

It was ten years after Pépère had died that I finally learned the secret. That brilliant summer evening, Mémère and I were sitting on the weathered back porch, she in a rocking chair and I on the wooden floor. I was working on my college reading, and she was sitting in unusual idleness, her gaze wandering over all the beauty of that wonderful little corner of the globe, the Saguenay.

I was in a bad mood that day because my car had broken down on the long drive from Montréal up to the farm. *Mon oncle* Alphonse and *mon oncle* Gédéon were dubious that it could fixed in time for my return down south, and I was furious at the wasted time, the inconvenient problem, and the upcoming financial toll. I was too frustrated to compose myself and study, huffing and puffing as I caught my book up and slammed it down again.

"You can't study with that attitude," Mémère said placidly as I dropped my book for the tenth time.

I mumbled something rebellious under my breath and immediately felt guilty, which didn't help my mood.

"*Jéhova-jiré*," she continued, quoting the Book she had spent so much of her life studying. "'L'Éternel y pourvoira.'"

Jehovah-jireh. The Lord will provide.

I groaned. "Wouldn't it be much better if He had kept this from happening so He wouldn't have to provide?"

"'Toutes choses concourent ensemble au bien de ceux qui aiment Dieu.'"

All things work together for good to them that love God. If I'd heard that once, I'd heard it a dozen times. It was Mémère's favourite verse, cliché as it was.

I must have made a doubtful face, because Mémère laughed a little. "You remind me of how I was at your age," she said with a sigh.

Mémère, rebellious and doubting God? It was impossible. She was such a holy, joyful woman, so trusting of the Lord she'd served faithfully all her life.

"Have you ever noticed that old red car over there?"

I perked up. "*Oui*, many times."

"And wondered why it's there?" Mémère added with a slight smile.

"Oui."

Mémère leaned back in her chair, and her eyes fastened unseeingly on the car with the look of one far away in bygone times. "I will tell you the story of that car. Many years ago…"

Jane Etta sighed as she tugged on her doorhandle. *This car is falling to pieces. But without Lester…*

The door gave way, and she staggered back on her high heels. Catching herself, she threw her pocketbook into the passenger seat and slipped into the car, slamming the door behind her. She closed her eyes and massaged her temples. It was only five-o'clock, but she was already drained. Working as a receptionist had never been her plan; but then, neither had a world-wide war.

"Wait for *meeee!*"

The girlish shriek rang out in the street and Jane Etta rolled her eyes, snatching back her pocketbook as Sandra whipped open the passenger door and popped in.

"It's so bright out there; I could never walk home in this glare. I'd go stark staring blind!"

Sandra giggled and settled herself in a great rustle. Jane Etta sourly ignored her. She was in no mood to deal with Sandra's overdone makeup, ridiculous hairstyle, and expensive, daring new outfit. Jane Etta felt a sudden unkind pride in her own sensible skirt-suit and hat. At least *she* was fairly decent, even if she *had* allowed herself the weakness of heels.

Ensuring that her skirt was loose and allowed her legs movement, she started the motor and pulled away from the office with a clunky roar.

"They'll hear us coming *blocks* away," Sandra said with another giggle. "You should call this car *Rachel Lynde*."

Jane Etta did not respond. The sun's rays outside and Sandra's brightness inside mocked her mood. Why couldn't it be grey and drizzly instead, like in the novels? Why couldn't Sandra be glum and silent? Sunshine belonged in the past; laughter had no part in the present.

The sun is always shining behind the clouds.

Jane Etta rolled her eyes. *Right. "You just have to look past the clouds to see it—and pretty soon it shows up again." Isn't that so, Lest?*

Too bad her cousin couldn't hear her sarcastic answers to his gentle rebukes that echoed in her memory.

"Coming to the lecture tonight?"

"No," Jane Etta retorted brusquely. Sandra knew better than to invite her out after work.

"Oh, Janey, it would do you good," Sandra protested. "You're too glum. You're like a—a Miss Havisham!"

Jane Etta's eyebrows rose in spite of herself. She hadn't expected Sandra to even know about *Great Expectations*, let alone the characters thereof. A mental prick startled her conscience. Once upon a time, she'd considered Miss Havisham ridiculous. Now, she understood the woman. Did that make her… *bad?*

She quickly smothered the thought.

"You know Miss Havisham, right?" Sandra pressed. "Mona said you were practically the world's foremost expert on classics. Dickens is a classic, isn't he? He's long-winded enough to be…"

Jane Etta almost smirked cynically before she caught herself. As a child, books and daydreams had filled her days. She'd tramped Sherwood with Robin Hood, defended Scotland with Sir William Wallace, sailed the seas with

78

Ishmael, solved mysteries with Sherlock Holmes, explored islands with Robinson Crusoe. She and her older brother Jimsy had run all over London together, scaling roofs and clearing buildings at a leap as they hunted down criminals and foiled enemy spies. The adventures they'd shared shone in her memory like a golden coin in a box of brass pennies. A long-submerged recollection arose…

"What ho, m'lady! Art going to His Majesty's banquet tonight?"

"Aye, good sir. Art thou?"

"Indeed, madam. May I have the honour of attending your most precious self?"

"My grateful thanks, Sir James."

"And me too, Sir Jimsy?"

"Yes, indeed, Miss Anne. How old art now?"

"I'm nearly eight!"

"A most precocious and avant-garde sister, m'lady."

"Indeed, sir. She is most deaf to the lessons of our good teacher."

"I can't talk like Netta can, Jimsy!"

"Don't cry, pet, you'll learn. May I have your arm, Miss Anne? And you, m'lady Jane?"

"Are you Jane Grey who's going to be beheaded, Netta?"

"No, I'm only simple Lady Jane… ah… Reginald."

"These are the castle stairs. Watch your steps, m'ladies. This fog is most dastardly…"

"Jimsy, I want a cloak like yours!"

"Art cold, miss? Allow me…"

"We should make more cloaks, Jimsy! Then we'd all have some!"

"Most clever of you, I'm sure, miss."

"Are we playing Medieval Scotland or are we playing

Victorian Britain? That's my train, Jim; don't step on it!"

"Sorry, sis—I mean, m'lady. Welcome to the banquet hall. What ho, minstrels! Strike up. Do not fear the gentlemen on the stairs, madams—they are loyal knights dedicated to your service and protection. A letter...? Thank you, Thomas. Ah—His Majesty is unable to attend tonight. We must join him at Guildhall tomorrow."

"That's in London, sir!"

"I crave your pardon, m'lady; I am afraid that my geography is somewhat weak. Thomas, bring a parchment; I must write to the King at once!"

"Let's seal it with Granny's old ring, Jimsy! We'll be the Scarlet Pimpernel sending orders to Sir Andrew."

The half-smile that had begun in Jane Etta's soul faded as tendrils of bitterness wrapped around the slender joyous stem, crushing out its life. The Spanish Flu had no mercy for even healthy, happy twenty-year-old brothers. Life was cruel.

"You know *Great Expectations*, right?"

Sandra was a human mosquito in persistence and noise, if not in looks.

"Yes," Jane Etta snapped.

Sandra settled her purse higher up on her lap and was quiet. Jane Etta was perversely pleased.

The cornfields were a mass of gently waving green and gold. It wasn't long until harvest, when the world would throb and roar with the machines.

I hate corn.

Her conscience pricked again. *Not really. I just hate anything that bothers my personal comfort.* She grimaced at the thought.

"How did you come here, Jane?"

"Do I *look* like I want to talk right now, Sandra?" Jane

Etta burst.

"No, but you look like you need to," Sandra giggled. "What brought you out here?"

"A train," Jane Etta said shortly.

"Why?"

"Because I needed money!" Jane Etta's voice was rising, and she didn't care.

"Natch," Sandra retorted airily. "The boss doesn't pay us enough for that. You came out here running away from something, Jane Etta Danson."

Jane Etta grimaced. Before her mind's eye old memories were flashing—memories of a heart-rending funeral; of a night seething in rage and pain; of silent goodbyes drenched by loved ones' reproachful tears; of a fiercely silent train ride across the country, fleeing... fleeing... fleeing... what? Why?

Jonah.

The words stung. She wasn't a Jonah... *or was she?* No, she had to think of something else. They were pulling into the farmyard now—

An ear-splitting shriek pierced her consciousness as Sandra snatched Jane Etta's arm and jerked it from the steering wheel. Screaming back, Jane Etta slammed the brakes and glared wildly for whatever she had—or nearly had—hit.

"*Looook!* Isn't he *handsome?*"

Jane Etta groaned and hid her face, collapsing like a jelly removed from its mold. "Sandra Byrd," she said fiercely, "if you frightened me out of a year's growth just to drool over a *Tommy*—"

A masculine voice interrupted her lecture. "Hardly much of a growth, O fierce and little Hermia, and greatly to be lamented. But for the sake of a clean atmosphere, *don't* call us Canucks 'Tommies.' I'm not particularly fond of 'blue' air."

Jane Etta dropped her hands and gasped.

"Furthermore, I am aware of your former instructions to come back 'with my shield or on it,' but unfortunately, the Canadian army's shields are alarmingly unfit for even my humble size—"

"Lester, Lester!" Miracle of miracles, the car door gave way at the first frantic tug, and Jane Etta tumbled into her cousin's uniformed arms, as hysterical as is proper for a heroine.

"Hello to you too, coz…" Lester grinned and hugged her briefly, then pushed her back and scrubbed at the mud staining his jacket. "Fences," he explained apologetically. "They have just as much of a vendetta out here as they did back home."

"I thought you were in Ontario shipping out!" Jane Etta cried.

"As the immortal Philippa said, 'Quote me correctly, honey.' My exact words were, 'I suppose I shall be sent to Ontario or someplace East to ship out.' As this stolid East is rather as vast a place as our own Wild West, I ended up in *la belle province*, in the army base not far from this charming French-Canadian town which, by the way, is a preparatory saunter through Germany. Delightful people, though, albeit what they don't say in German wouldn't cumber a fly."

"You and your ridiculous metaphors," Jane Etta said with fond tolerance, brushing more mud off his jacket.

Lester raised a forefinger to emphasize a pompous speech, backed up for proper effect, tripped over a loose log, staggered wildly, and collapsed onto his back, his glasses sliding neatly down to the edge of his nose. Behind them, Sandra screeched her laughter and rocked to and fro on her high heels.

With a resigned sigh, Lester scrambled to his feet, wiped his hands on his pants, and offered one to Sandra, giving Jane Etta the long-suffering look of a martyr who had been dragged to the stake as the finishing touch to an inauspicious day.

"Lester Ford," he said, blinking in placid fortitude.

"Sandra Byrd," Jane Etta introduced them ungraciously, as Sandra seized Lester's hand and pulled it close.

"Pleased to meet you, I'm sure," Lester murmured, telegraphing an agonized appeal to Jane Etta. She reached out and took his arm, jerking him away from her coworker.

"Would you like a guide through town?" Sandra cooed, ignoring Jane Etta and batting her eyelashes at Lester, her over-red lips pursed in an affected pout.

"No... plans..." Lester stammered, wildly uncomfortable and forgetting every word he ever knew. "Coz...?" He looked helplessly and hopefully at Jane Etta.

"We'll see you later, Sandra," Jane Etta said crisply, leading Lester towards her car. Sandra's attractive pose disappeared in a flash as she shot Jane Etta a venomous glare.

"Where are we going?" Jane Etta asked, as soon as Lester had closed the car door upon them.

"For someone so sure of herself, you sound remarkably lost," murmured Lester, adjusting his glasses and avoiding Sandra, who stood by the farmyard gate staring, and plainly had no intention of going into the house until the other two had submitted to taking her along—or left.

Jane Etta rolled her eyes. "I rescued you from a predicament you were too polite to end yourself. Where are you taking me?"

"Does dinner and a lecture sound like sufficient

payment?" Lester asked meekly.

"But I told Sandra I wasn't going."

"Then I shall have demonstrated my sublime persuasion skills. By the way, that charming friend of yours shall fly away someday," Lester added in annoyance, accidentally making eye contact with Sandra and setting off another burst of eye-batting.

"I don't understand why she hasn't already," Jane Etta said sarcastically. "I swear her eyelashes get longer every week, and her head is a perfect balloon as far as emptiness goes."

"And from that Cupid's bow came the banshee-worthy shriek that would have frightened Napoleon back into his bed and saved Moscow?"

Jane Etta laughed in spite of herself, and Lester grinned proudly. "I understand, however, that she was the means of you getting this triumphal chariot, for which I bow to her with my hand on my heart. Mrs. Morphe told me the story of the Geezer."

"Give an old boy some respect. He's toughed out more things than you," Jane Etta returned severely.

"Not to strengthen the stereotype, fair coz, but your old boy looks like he *could* use some work," Lester retorted, wrestling wildly with the motor and knocking his glasses nearly off his face.

"Not to strengthen the stereotype, but I'm hopeless playing Rosie the Riveter," Jane Etta mumbled.

"Nothing a few knocks with a screwdriver won't fix," Lester said, brightening.

"It won't hurt, anyways," Jane Etta answered gloomily.

"Cheer up, coz. How do fries and a burger sound as balm to an afflicted mind? Mind you, I recently learned that

French fries are *not* French but Belgian. The usual anglophone misunderstanding, of course..."

The evening was still and golden. Far in the west, the sun still held night at bay. Crickets and frogs sang in harmony, with the wind whistling the tune.

Seated at the outside table, Jane Etta hummed along to the smooth waves of piano and violin floating out from the radio inside the restaurant.

"Remember our first piano lesson?"

Jane Etta rolled her eyes, but a small smile forced its way to her lips. Lester's earnest but verbose, over-complicated instructions; her own impatient, irritable disposition; and an audience of merry little siblings was not a recipe for success. An old-fashioned squabble had ensued, in which Lester had forgotten both dignity and vocabulary and Jane Etta had recourse to the usual feminine weapon—tears.

"I haven't played in forever," she said, taking the last French fry.

"Really, ma'am, you're ruining my reputation as a teacher," Lester began, snatching at the fry and breaking off half. Jane Etta snorted.

The piano piece ended, and a waltz began crooning through the air. Lester grinned.

"Still good on your toes?"

"Better than you, soldier."

"That's a challenge."

Before she could protest, they were standing hand in hand, holding each other's shoulders and swaying gently to the dreamy melody.

"You *have* gotten remarkably kinder to my toes," Jane Etta said graciously.

"Poor Aunt Margie's feet were not sacrificed in vain. How *is* the dear woman, and all the 'folks back home'?"

Jane Etta stiffened, which was not conducive to graceful dancing. "Oh, they're all right," she answered vaguely. "I don't hear from them very often, you know. Dreadfully busy."

"You mean you don't write to them, do you?" Lester said shrewdly.

Jane Etta frowned and gave up on dancing altogether. She pulled away from Lester and ran petulantly back to her seat. When he came over and sat back down, she turned her back more squarely upon him. The silence was uncomfortable.

"It's nice out here," Lester said suddenly, his voice unusually thoughtful. "Hard to think that across the world, murder is happening within these very same surroundings…"

Jane Etta shivered unexpectedly. Perhaps it was cliché, but she had always understood when book characters drank in nature and reflected with amazement on the wickedness of mankind. She'd never expected to experience this herself… but then, what was fiction but pictures of life, after all?

"Who would have thought, when we said goodbye last fall, where we'd meet again?" Lester mused on. "I admit that I was frankly disgusted at being put here and gave the Lord an earful about it at first. Never guessed I'd run into you. Isn't it a splendid reminder that everything turns out to our good?"

"That's not the right words," Jane Etta mumbled, trying to stave off the oncoming exhortation. She *had* been wishing for him only a little while ago… but that must be merely a coincidence.

"I wasn't quoting the verse, merely stating a fact. Really, coz, the older I get, the more I see the 'bad' things that happened to me aren't so bad after all, since the Lord turns them into such glorious things."

"What about Jimsy?" Jane Etta demanded fiercely. "What about Uncle Perry?"

Lester's lips whitened, but his voice remained steady.

"Father's death *was* terrible. But good still came out of it, Netta. It was at his funeral that poor old Jerome was saved... and you know how Father prayed over *him*."

"And Jimsy?" Jane Etta cried. "You can't find any good in *Jimsy's* death, Lester Ford!"

"Jimsy's death kept him safe, Jane Etta," Lester said sturdily, locking gazes with her. "The Good Lord knew it was best for him to go. The work he had to do here was done, and it was time for him to enter his reward. If he had stayed, it wouldn't have been good for him. I firmly believe that, Netta. That's why I can surrender Father and Jimsy and the others who've died around me, because I *know* they are more blessed now than I can possibly imagine; they are happy and peaceful; and this is the best thing that could ever happen to them. I love them enough to want the best for them... and I know the Lord'll take care of the ones who are left behind—which He *has*, if you only look for it."

"*Everything* cannot turn to our good," Jane Etta hissed.

"Would you rather believe that than believe that it *does*?" Lester demanded. "Would you rather live in the hope that whatever hardship you're in will someday be worth something? Or would you rather just think that the pain is pointless and merely a blind chance that torments you forever?"

A sudden illustration filled Jane Etta's mind. *Two paths littered with stones and pierced with holes, running along a high cliff that bordered a frightening chasm. Over each hung a dark raincloud, making the paths dangerously slick.*

But along one path ran a rope, rough but sturdy, to cling to when one's feet gave way. And peering down this path, one saw the clouds shift a little, giving comforting glimpses of blue skies or bright rainbows.

Jane Etta blinked, and the image faded from her mind. She put a hand to her heart. Did she *really* want to go down the path without the safety rope, the path where the raincloud had no promise of ending?

"Lester," she said desperately, "I *don't* want to. But I can't *see* how anything good has possibly come from all the bad things that have happened to me—the fire, that school, Abbie…"

"Faith doesn't work by sight, Netta," Lester said quietly. "You just have to *believe* that it is so because you trust the One who said it."

"Just like I believe the rope will hold me even if I can't see that it will, just because I trust the ones who put it up," Jane Etta whispered to herself.

"It's hard," Lester admitted. "I know it's hard. But it's doable… and it's worth it… and He's trustworthy, Netta."

He shrugged eloquently, words failing his earnestness. He could do no more. This choice she must make herself, in her own heart.

"I hope I can, Lest," she choked through rising tears, feeling that this was indeed a momentous occasion.

Lester was silent for a moment, then he took her hands in his. "Lord," he whispered, "please open her eyes and her heart."

Jane Etta bowed her head, echoing his prayer. *Please, Lord… show me Your redemption of my pain.*

And as Lester wrapped his own arms around her, giving the comfort she'd yearned after for so many weary months, a whisper slipped through her mind.

He already has.

Mémère fell silent, lost in the past, and I stared at her in silence. I had never known much about her early life, but I had never considered what it held. I had never guessed that Christ-centred Jeannette Beaumont, the hardworking farmer's wife and loving mother of twelve, had ever been bitter, broken Jane Etta Danson, a western preacher's runaway daughter.

"And that car is The Geezer?" I asked softly, hesitant to disturb Mémère but wishing for an ending to the story.

Mémère nodded slowly. "That is The Geezer," she said. "Lester managed to fix a few things before he shipped out, and afterwards one of the young men from the church I joined helped me make a couple other repairs. His name was Jérôme."

I grinned, recognizing Pépère's name.

"The Geezer plodded faithfully along for fifteen long years. Every so often it would break down, right when we could least afford repairs. But every time God sent the ways and means, and The Geezer went on. Then when someone gave us a newer car, The Geezer stopped working for good. I couldn't bear to let it go, so Jérôme put it in the pasture, and it's been there ever since, reminding me every time I see it that God truly works everything together for my good. Of course, it took a long time for me to change, and I'm still so imperfect. I've fallen so many times, I've worried and cried and questioned, but He's never failed me once, and in spite of everything I've been through, I can still say, He is good, He is faithful, and He makes things better than I could ever imagine them."

Mémère closed her eyes, and I saw her lips move, whispering a prayer to the Confidant and Guide who'd walked with her up so many mountains and down through so many valleys. The setting sun gleamed on the roof of The Geezer. Winters and springs, summers and autumns had passed, each leaving their mark on the valiant red car. Over it days had dawned and nights had fallen, many more than I could ever count. It had seen planting-times of simple faith and harvest-times of plenteous rewards. The old promise had remained true: "While the earth remaineth, seedtime and harvest, and cold and heat, and summer and winter, and day and night shall not cease." A simple promise, yet one full of power.

God proved His word true every day around me. Each breath of life that filled my lungs cried out His faithfulness. In the galaxy of gigantic stars and aligned planets He ruled, I was only an infinitesimal speck on the great globe He had created so lovingly for me and mine. Yet He saw me, He knew me, He upheld me, and He listened to me. My problems were so small in my sight as I measured His infinity, yet to Him they were important and worth taking care of.

He loved me so.

How could I but trust Him?

EVERYTHING
BY LILLY WISCAVER

*This story is dedicated to Sierra Ruga. The Lord has been so good,
even in the fire.*

Chapter 1

EMILY HOPPED ON her bed in an unladylike manner. Not that
she cared, because her bedroom door was closed and her
mother didn't see her. Even though she was sixteen,
sometimes she didn't act like she was, especially when she was
in her own bedroom.

What else do I need to pack? she wondered. In less than
two days, her family, Lord willing, would be heading to a
country in the Middle East to smuggle Bibles. Because of
that, several items of her clothing were things she normally
wouldn't wear here in the US.

Her dad wasn't thrilled with the idea of his wife and
daughter having to dress like everyone else in the country. He
felt they were trying to hide the fact they were Christians.

After long talks with the missionaries in that Middle Eastern country and some deacons at their church, they decided it would be best while they were smuggling the Bibles. The Bible smuggling would only be for a short time, and Bible smuggling was very dangerous.

Anyone caught with a Bible was tortured and sometimes executed. While the Stone family didn't want to hide the fact they were Christians and weren't afraid of persecution, they knew the Christians in the Middle East desperately needed the Bible. They knew persecution spread the Gospel; they knew blending in to smuggle the Bibles was also important.

Some people didn't agree with the Stone family's decision, but Emily knew they weren't doing it for themselves, but for the people of the country. She had heard how thirsty they were to have a single copy of the Bible.

"Emily!" a voice called, followed by a knock on her bedroom door. Emily quickly snapped out of her thoughts and opened her door.

"Come in, Travis," she replied to her twin brother.

"I was wondering if you'd ever answer the door," he teased. "Dad wanted to know if your suitcase could hide three more Bibles. Everyone else's suitcases are full already, so if not, we may have to find someplace else to put them."

"I have a bit of room, but I know I'll think of other things I'll need to bring with me," Emily replied, taking the Bibles from Travis' hands.

"Girls. They always have more stuff than us men," Travis said with a shrug.

"Well, you must remember we're taking everything we need for this two-week trip with us. Sometimes us girls have more stuff than we like."

"Yeah, and girls have a tendency to always forget

something," he teased.

"Whatever you say, little brother." Emily gave him a small, playful smirk, though both Travis and she knew he was right.

"I am not your little brother, and you know that."

"Five whole minutes; you're older than me by five whole minutes."

"Why don't I leave you to finish packing? I need to check to make sure I have everything I need," Travis decided, changing the subject.

"Same here," Emily replied, looking at the packing list she had made. Bible, check. Clothes, check. Hairbrush, check.

Thirty minutes later, she decided she had everything she would need for the trip as well as a little extra.

Chapter 2

One and a half weeks later

"Well, we have these packages to distribute farther in, and after that, we can go to the house," Dad said, in-between reading the map. Their driver wasn't a Christian, so they had to be careful what they said in front of him. He didn't speak English very well, but they didn't want to risk having the Bibles and Christian literature taken.

They prayed for the driver as he drove and tried to ask him some indirect questions on what he thought of Christians, if he'd ever leave the beliefs he'd grown up with, and so forth. Unlike in America, it was harder to witness to people in this Middle Eastern country. Most of the natives thought Christians were infidels and should not be allowed to live here, whether that meant not in this country or put to death.

"Yay!" Emily exclaimed, excited she'd be able to see her friend Kathryn again, along with help at the mission house. "It'll be nice to catch up with Kathryn before we leave again."

"How many days until we have to catch our plane?" Emily's younger brother, Cole, asked.

"I think we have four days," Mom told her son.

"This not good," the driver said with a thick accent.

"What's not good?" Emily's dad asked, looking up from the map.

"Milit'ry. People don't obey religion." Emily glanced at her dad and mother, then at her brothers. They knew exactly what their driver was talking about. The military would drag anyone who professed to be a Christian on the street. They had heard stories about new Christians who had stood boldly for their beliefs and didn't reject the name of Christ.

Everyone, particularly females, who didn't abide by the dress code was punished. Sometimes that meant a severe beating, but oftentimes it was far worse. The Christians didn't fear death, but they did fear torture. The missionaries were overjoyed that many of the new Christians were willing to follow Christ no matter what and didn't recant during the torture.

"We turn around," the driver said. "No way through."

"There's not another route we can take?" Dad asked.

"No other route," the driver confirmed, turning the car around.

I'm sure there's another route, Emily thought. *I'm pretty sure the driver is just scared of the military.*

Dad looked nervously at Mom. *Should I press the driver?*

94

he seemed to ask. Emily saw her dad bow his head and move his mouth slightly. Emily did the same. She knew how important these Bibles were to these new Christians, and they were willing to give everything for the cause of Christ. After what seemed an eternity, Emily heard her dad's voice.

"I am willing to pay you extra," he told the driver, "if you can get us to our destination."

"How much?" the driver asked, suddenly interested.

Emily's dad named a high price, almost a whole day's wages in this country.

"Well," the driver said, "another route is near, but bumpy. We go on it."

"We'll be fine; it doesn't matter to us if the road is bumpy. Just get us to our destination, please." The driver turned the car around again and navigated it to some backroad. *Thank you, Lord!* Emily prayed silently. She was willing to risk everything for the cause of Christ because the Christians in this foreign land were willing to risk everything for the cause of Christ.

Two hours later, the five Stones were back at the mission house, praising God for the opportunity to deliver the Bibles to the hungry Christians. One of the Christians who would distribute the Bibles cried so hard when the Stones gave them to him. He said he had never held a copy of the Bible in his hands before.

Emily was so touched by how desperately these people had wanted a copy of the Bible. She knew these people would only get one Bible and would have to share with their families or church. Emily herself had two Bibles. One was a worn-out one she had received when she was a young girl, and the other one was a newer one, which she currently used.

Chapter 3

"What has been the most interesting part of visiting here?" Kathryn asked, as the girls prepared for bed.

Emily plucked the hairpins out of her hair as she tried to think of an answer for Kathryn. "Probably seeing how desperate the Christians here are for a single copy of the Bible or how they're willing to risk everything for the cause of Christ. I feel guilty for having two copies of the Bible when a community of believers here might have one copy. I've been asking myself if I'd be willing to give up everything—my family, my possessions, my way of life—for the cause of Christ."

"Are you willing to lose everything for the cause of Christ?"

Emily hesitated. She had asked herself this question for a long time, since she became a Christian four years ago.

"Yes, I am willing to lose everything for Christ's sake. He will provide everything I need, and He's all I need."

"'Yea doubtless, and I count all things but loss for the excellency of the knowledge of Christ Jesus my Lord: for whom I have suffered the loss of all things, and do count them but dung, that I may win Christ.' That's Philippians 3:8."

The girls crawled into bed, but Emily couldn't sleep.

Yes, she told herself, *I would be willing to follow Christ even if that meant losing everything. It might be difficult, but Christ means that much to me. What was it Job said? 'The LORD gave, and the LORD hath taken away; blessed be the name of the LORD.' (Job 1:21) Everything is the Lord's, and He can take it away anytime.*

Emily figured she wouldn't have to worry about losing everything for being a Christ follower, but she knew it was highly possible she would lose something for being His follower. She knew all her possessions were just things. Most of it didn't mean much to her, except her Bible. But even if she lost her physical copy of the Bible, she had so much tucked away in her mind.

"That's odd. Our flight is canceled." Emily looked up from her bags to her dad.

"Really?" her mom asked.

"Yes. It was rescheduled to next week. I guess we'll be staying here for another week."

"Well, the mission house needs help, so I guess we need to surrender everything we had planned and give it to God," Emily's mom said.

Everything is the Lord's, Emily thought. *Even our time. It's all His.*

Chapter 4

The Stones stayed in the Middle East for another

week. They helped with the mission house, did some evangelism, distributed another shipment of Bibles, and best of all, Emily no longer wore the same clothes the natives there did.

She was allowed to dress in the dresses she loved most. Bible smuggling was dangerous, and they wanted to make sure the new Christians had access to at least a copy of the Word, but since that was over now, the Stones weren't in as much danger. Being a Christian was dangerous enough, but they knew being a Christian didn't mean life would be nice and full of wealth and happiness.

"Goodbye," Kathryn whispered as she and Emily parted. "Are you still willing to lose everything for Christ's sake?"

Emily nodded. "I most certainly am. Coming here and seeing the Christians here was such an inspiration to me. It also made me realize how blessed I am to have been raised in a land where being a Christian isn't a crime and to have a family who raised me in the fear of God."

"I agree, Emily. Before Dad and Mom decided to be missionaries here, I didn't understand how blessed we were when we lived in the States and how believers in other countries lost everything and suffered for being a Christian. I've changed a lot since we moved here seven years ago. All for the better too." The girls hugged again, then Emily joined her family, ready to board the plane.

Over fifteen hours later, the Stones arrived in New Jersey. The weather was hot and dry. Emily had heard that there were lots of fires because of the extreme drought.

"Our plane isn't taking off for another three hours," her dad said, returning to the benches where they were seated. "They accidently overbooked the plane we were supposed to take, and they offered us five hundred dollars to take the next flight.

"Not a bad deal," Travis stated. "We could divide the money up. One hundred dollars per person for food."

Emily laughed. Her brother loved to good-naturedly tease, and he was always thinking about food, like most teenaged boys.

"I think there's a deli in this airport." Mr. Stone pulled out the airport map. "Yep, it's right here." He turned to his wife and daughter. "What would you two like to eat?"

After three long hours at the airport and another three hours on the plane, Emily and her family were almost home. Emily herself was nearly asleep when her dad's cell phone broke the silence.

"Hello?" Turning to his wife, he quietly asked her to put the phone on speaker, since he was driving.

"Hello, is this Daniel Stone of Montgomery, Indiana?"

"Yes, this is him."

"This is Sheriff Conner Hammond of the Daviess County Sheriff's department. Is your residence 18796 CR 142?"

"Yes, it is."

"I don't know how to say this, Mr. Stone, but this morning, your house caught on fire. Everything is gone. There's nothing left but ashes." Emily sat up. Was she dreaming?

"We're actually on our way home from a three-week trip. We'll be there in about two hours. Can you tell me any other information?"

"Well, the fire started around midnight. The fire department was actually fighting another house fire, so they had to get it under control before they were able to go to your home. By the time they got there, the whole house was in flames. The fire chief is still determining the cause and where it started."

"Wow. Praise the Lord we weren't home."

"Yes, praise the Lord indeed." Several minutes passed before the sheriff hung up.

"Did we hear him correctly?" Travis asked.

"I believe we did," Dad replied.

"Beauty for ashes," Emily whispered.

"What?" Cole asked.

"Beauty for ashes. I was reading my Bible this morning at the airport, and I was in the passage that said 'beauty for ashes.'"

Chapter 5

The Stones drove down the lane to their house. The trees blocked their view. Emily was wondering if everything they had, aside from what was with them on the trip, was really gone. Rounding the bend, she saw their house. Or rather, what was left of it. It was all gone. Nothing was standing. All was a pile of ashes.

"It really is gone," she heard her mother say in a low voice. Exiting the car, they were all eager to see if anything was left in all these ruins.

"It's really all gone." Dad's voice broke the silence.

"It's just stuff," Emily heard herself reply.

"Yes, it is," her dad agreed. "We can praise the Lord we were not home when it happened."

"I wonder if we would have survived if we had been here. It looks like everything is in ashes." Travis scanned the ground.

"I don't know," Dad replied. "I think the Lord saved us for a reason. I believe He delayed our plane so we wouldn't be here."

"Do you think we can find anything under these ashes?" Cole asked.

"Well, there's only one way to find out, Son. Let's take a look." The five Stones made their way to a shed that was still standing. Inside, they found some shovels.

"Do you think all of our money is gone?" Emily heard her mother ask.

"I don't know." Her dad scanned the location where the dresser would have been. Emily's family didn't like banks. They were a bit old-fashioned, but recent news had prompted them to move a good deal of money from the bank to their house. They knew their money could have been stolen or burnt in a fire, but they knew that if the Lord decided they didn't need the money, He could take it away from them anytime.

"What'd you find, Cole?" Emily called out to her brother, who was stooped over and picking something up.

"Em, look!" He cried out. She carefully made her way to her younger brother.

"Is that…" She gulped. It couldn't be. "Is that my…"

Cole nodded as Emily reached out to grab the wooden box. Emily wasn't a sentimental person, but her grandpa had made this box for her before she was born. She had never met her mother's dad, but from what she had heard from her mom and grandma, she knew she would have loved being around him.

"That is really neat your box survived." Cole kept moving ashes around.

"How could our whole house burn down yet a wooden box survives?" she said aloud to no one in particular. Lifting the lid, she carefully scanned the box. A tear slid down her cheek as she realized everything was intact.

At the top of the box was a package of brand-new tracts she had bought right before they left for their trip. She carefully set the tracts down as she pulled the other items out. At the bottom of the box was every dollar she had to her name. Though it wasn't much, she knew she could buy the things she'd need most with it.

"Emily, look!" Travis held items in his hands that resembled books.

"What is it?"

Travis set the books in her hands for an answer. Emily turned the books over. One was a study Bible that had been gifted to them and the other book was a concordance.

"'The grass withereth, the flower fadeth: but the word of our God shall stand for ever,'" (Isaiah 40:8) Dad quoted. "Not even a fire can destroy the Word of our Lord." Tears were running down their faces as they thanked the Lord for His Word.

Emily handed the books to her mother and decided to walk across the ashes, hoping to find something. All she could see was ashes. She was amazed the Bible, concordance, and her wooden box had survived the flames. She knew that her Heavenly Father was watching out for her and providing for all of her needs.

"Hey you!" a new voice called, breaking her thoughts. She instantly recognized her friend, Joanna Weaver, who lived over an hour away. Joanna's family were leaving to be missionaries in a few weeks, and Emily didn't know if she'd be able to see her dear friend before they left.

"Joanna!" The two girls embraced as Joanna quickly explained that they were in the area when the Stones' pastor had called them. Joanna's church was a sister church to Emily's.

"Here, I want to show you something." Emily led Joanna to their vehicle where she had set her box. "Look, Joanna!"

"This survived the flames?" Joanna asked, amazed.

"Yes, it did. I like to think it was how God was showing me He was watching over me. Had our flight not been canceled, we probably would have gone to meet our Savior."

"I'd love to meet my Savior, but I will serve Him and follow Him until He calls me home."

"Amen." Emily sat the box back in the vehicle. "Want to come help me look through the ashes?"

"Of course. That is why Dad, Matthew, and I came." Joanna and Emily headed toward what had been the Stones' home for years.

"Were you in town to do something else?" Emily asked, as the girls brushed ashes from side to side.

"Yes, we needed to buy some items to repair the fence on the farm. We were at the lumber store when Brother David called. We had to pick up some items for Mother, too, while we were in town, but we wanted to come and see you all. Brother David said he was bringing some men from your church to help your dad decide what to do next and to figure out where you'll be staying."

"I hadn't even thought about where we would stay." Emily stooped down to pick up what looked like a twenty-dollar bill. "Joanna, is this what I think it is?"

Joanna looked up from where she had stooped down. "Yes, it is. Look what I found." She laid another bill into Emily's hand.

"I think this is Dad and Mother's money." Emily and Joanna carefully sifted through the ashes, wondering if they'd find more money.

It wasn't long before Joanna's brother, Matthew, came to join them, along with Cole.

"Here's another one." Matthew pulled another bill out from the ashes and handed it to Mrs. Stone. The bill was charred slightly on the edges, but otherwise, it was perfect.

Chapter 6

By the end of the day, the Stones had recovered most of their savings, with the help of many of their friends. They were in so much shock. The Lord was so good to them. Pastor David led the group in prayer, giving thanks for providing the Stones with so much already. Mr. Stone also thanked the Lord for His goodness. Even though they had so little compared to most people in the United States, they had much more than the people in the country they had just returned from. And they knew it.

"Bye, Joanna." Emily gave her friend a quick hug.

"Bye, Emily. Hopefully I'll get to see you again before

we leave."

"I hope we can. If not, I'll miss you, but I understand your family wants to go where the Lord leads."

"Yes, we do." Joanna smiled and waved as she returned to the van with her father and her brother.

Emily's heart was full and happy, as was her stomach. A family from their church, the Fishers, let the Stones use their house as the Fishers were on a two-week trip in Canada to visit extended family. As soon as they had heard the Stones' house caught on fire, they immediately told them where to find the spare key and to use their house until they returned. The Fishers had just started their trip to Canada, so the Stones had twelve days to stay in their house.

"That pizza was good," Travis remarked as he carried his dishes to the sink.

"Don't forget to thank Samuel Albert for ordering the pizza." Dad returned with his Bible.

"I won't forget," Travis, Emily, and Cole voiced in unison.

"Good. Let's thank the Lord for His goodness and how He has provided so much for us already." The Stones bowed their heads. "Lord, we gather together to thank you for sparing us in this fire. We know You could have taken us home, but You decided to keep us here to serve You. We don't know why you decided to let our house burn down, but we trust Your plan.

"You have provided so much for us already, and You have given us everything we need and so much more. Everything we have is Yours, Lord, and You give and take away. Thank You for providing for us, and please give us wisdom as to what we should do next. We know You will provide for us, and now we trust You to give us everything we need."

Emily lay in bed, pondering the day's events. She had never thought her house would burn down. She had lost nearly everything. Pictures from her childhood, neat things she had found, most of her clothes, books—everything. Yet she had so much. She had a roof over her head, a warm bed to sleep in, several changes of clothes, money to buy anything she really needed, and most importantly, a copy of the Bible. She had everything she truly needed.

"I have everything I need," she whispered. "Not only do I have physical things, but I have Christ, and He's everything I need. Even if I lost everything physical, I still have Him. The Lord allowed my family to be spared; He could have allowed my family and maybe myself to come home to Him in the fire, but He left us here.

"In the world's eyes, if I had lost all my possessions and my family, I would have lost everything. But I still would have Christ!" Emily's heart was happy, knowing that even if she had lost everything, including her family, she'd still have with her the One Who saved her. Nothing could make her more joyful.

Since she couldn't sleep, she decided to look up some Bible passages. Her gaze instantly fell to Psalm 34:9.

"O fear the LORD, ye His saints: for there is no want to them that fear Him." *Hm*, she wondered to herself, *there is no want to them that fear Him*. She thought about what that meant. Her mind went to Psalm 23:1.

"The Lord is my Shepherd; I shall not want." *The Lord truly is my everything. He supplies all my needs and gives me everything I need. I have everything I need. I lack nothing. Jesus is my everything.* A tear slipped down Emily's face. She had just lost almost everything. Yet the Lord was faithful to her, providing everything she and her family needed and so much more.

EVERYTHING
BY ERIKA MATHEWS

THE OLD BROWN shoebox and I had both seen better days. The box could hardly be called rectangular anymore; it was more of a saggy, nondescript, mostly four-sided object now. As I closed my eyes and stroked the cardboard with my fingers, the warm tingling in my heart reflected that of the first time I'd held this same box.

We hadn't seen better days then, the shoebox and me. No, that was our prime—the very herald of the best year of our lives. The box was pristine and new, and it kept safe the dainty white satin flats that would grace my feet as I spoke lifelong covenant vows to my Philip.

Those flats are long gone now, and so is Philip, the dear man. I wore them both out, I'm afraid. Philip and I had many happy years together, but the flats never made it back into the box.

Gingerly I nudged the lid aside. The box hadn't stayed empty. No, it overflowed with love. With memories.

I closed my eyes and inhaled the cinnamon scents contained within, the reminisces of nearly seventy-seven Christmases washing over me with the aroma. How many years had we made those cinnamon ornaments before the tradition faded?

With trembling fingers, I pulled aside tissue paper, and a round, milky-white Christmas ornament sat on my palm. I could still feel Philip's hands over mine the first time he placed this ornament within mine—and see that sincere smile in his brown eyes.

That first Christmas... It was his gift, that oversized pearly decoration. He said it represented the precious value of a grateful heart. His voice still echoed in my ears. "A pearl is formed through acceptance with joy, my dear. When an irritation—a grain of sand, a bit of shell, or a parasite—lodges inside the oyster's shell, instead of complaining and rejecting it, it accepts it, and that acceptance over many years builds layers that turn it into something beautiful. So too may you and I coat our irritations and sufferings in thankfulness and joy, and may those layers of thankfulness and joy build within us to create a pearl of great price."

I closed my eyes, heedless of the tears that welled up. My first Christmas without him. We'd had our share of irritations and sufferings, to be sure, but at least we'd faced them together.

This was without doubt my favorite part of the Christmas season, even if bittersweet. The memories. From the time the children were little, I'd always loved when the Christmas ornament box came down from the attic. Oh, how Beth and Jenny and David had danced and squealed and scampered about with every forgotten ornament unwrapped and hung! Even now, the house seemed to echo with their excited little voices. How many happy moments this room had captured!

Yet now... Never had my heart throbbed in so much grief or loneliness. Never had I had to open this box alone before. Never was Philip not here to laugh, cry, or sigh over our shared collection of a lifetime of living memories.

The little manger, crudely painted and dangling from a frayed ribbon... Little newborn Beth had been struggling with croup that year. How many sleepless nights I'd suffered worrying needlessly about her! If only I had learned to fully trust much earlier in life the One who had kept His own Son in that manger. I'm afraid the irritants in my life from that season hadn't become much of a pearl.

Little clay handprints... What a delight those little hands had been! How many of those very same handprints had I scrubbed off the walls, the windows, the doors, the cupboards, even the ceiling!

Off of everything.

That had been Beth's first word, after Mama and Dadda. "Ev-ee-sing," she'd pronounced it. Lying in her crib on those dark evenings before she was two, she'd murmur to herself, "In ev-ee-sing give sanks."

Ah, and here was the set of blue ornaments I'd finally received as a gift several years into motherhood. I couldn't even look at them without remembering the time that Jenny had thought it would be funny to hang them on her ears— and the ears of everyone else in the family. Her howls when one of the ornaments slipped, smashed, and cut her finger still rang in *my* ears. "Give thanks," Beth had yelled above Jenny's wailings. "This is part of everything."

"This is part of everything," I repeated now, wrapping my hand around the smallest one and lifting my teary face upward. "This is part of everything. I thank You."

And I grinned, for wouldn't Philip have said the same? If he hadn't, Beth certainly would have reminded us. What a treasure that girl was. Still is. If only she were able to get furlough to come for Christmas this year... Longing tugged at my heart, longing stronger than I'd felt in a long time. I missed her, even though I wouldn't have her leave her mission work for anything.

"This is part of everything," I repeated. "Thank You that she is listening to You and leading so many darkened souls into Your Light."

Ornament after ornament I unwrapped and gazed upon, my thoughts far in the past. There were the marks where Jenny had bitten the wooden snowflake as a baby. Ah, Jenny. Why hadn't I pulled out this box last week when she was here? She could have gone through these with me. Next time she would come, the box would be packed back in the attic. Christmas was always quieter the year Jenny spent it with her husband's family. Jenny was the outgoing one, the talkative one, the joy and the life of the party.

This is part of everything. I hung the snowflake on the tree next to me. "Thank You that You have given her a loving husband and his wonderful family. Thank You for giving her to me."

Here were the homemade cinnamon gingerbread men, some of whom were missing arms or legs. I cradled one limbless ornament in my hands, my eyes closing as I pursed my lips and inhaled deeply.

God *was* still good, even when I felt exactly like this worn ornament. Part of me felt missing.

But He would never leave me nor forsake me.

And this was part of everything.

Now those words sing-songing in my head belonged to all three of my children together. Somehow, despite my many failings, God had taught them well. And they'd taught *me*.

Thank You. Another piece of tissue paper unwrapped under my fingers.

Mr. Scary. I'd never forget the ridiculous name David had given the scarecrow he'd made in fourth grade—nor how I'd struggled to conceal my distaste when he'd proudly presented it to me. For years, in fact, I'd shuddered to see it on the Christmas tree, and I'd always tried to hide it in the back—but, of course, my happy little son always moved it front and center.

It had taken far too long for me to start making *that* irritation into a pearl.

Now David no doubt played "Mr. Scary" with his own five lively children as he tucked them into bed every night. I'd hoped to at least see him for Christmas this year, but his wife's chronic illnesses always made travel so uncertain, especially during the cold months. David had said December had seemed exceptionally poor so far. Perhaps one day they'd be able to live closer...

I sighed. *This is part of everything.*

"Thank You, Yahweh, that David is such a devoted husband and father to his family. Thank You for giving him a wife to love, cherish, and care for. And thank You for blessing them with children. How blessed I am to have such a fine son and such precious grandchildren!"

I drew in a deep breath, feeling the loneliness within ease a bit as a gentle calm swept in. How blessed I was that my children were following the one true God! What was a bit of temporary loneliness, even at Christmastime, to the thought of eternity together with them!

And with Philip.

This is part of everything.

I tightened my lips and plunged my hand back into the shoebox. I didn't want to think of that—not yet. I *knew* I needed to thank God for Philip and his... absence... but I just couldn't. Not yet. I wanted to... but...

Heedless of where my fingers landed, I pulled out another ornament.

I caught my breath.

My children. Baptized together. Receiving the outward symbol of their inner surrender to Yahweh. The tears that I'd kept inside spilled out, baptizing me and the box in the beauty and refreshment of the sacred memory. I could see myself again there in my best dress and my shoes sinking into the mud down at the creek behind Farmer Roadstrom's barn, my right hand clutching a birch sapling as my heart pounded with joy as first Beth, then Jenny, then David entered the water and Philip baptized them. Even now, my heart throbbed with the overflowing joy I'd felt then. Philip's gigantic grin, more joyful than I'd ever seen it before. Which was saying a lot, since it's Philip we're talking about. Beth's tender smile that radiated joy and peace. The water dripping off Jenny's braids, her crooked grin spilling out and her feet refusing to stay still in her exuberance. David's smile—a real smile—directed right at me. The butterfly that landed on the back of my hand. The way the breeze tossed the branches and Beth shivered in her towel. The sly side-glance Jenny shot me as she opened her hand to reveal the clay she'd yanked from the creek bottom on her way up out of the water… the same clay that formed the plaque in my hand—the date etched into it along with the figures of three shining pearls.

I couldn't wait then to see how God would use their lives—and now! Oh, He'd done so much more than I could ask or think. Even through Jenny's terrifying accident, through Beth's tragic miscarriages, and David's uncertainties with his wife's health, God had never forsaken them, and they had never forsaken Him.

Truly, I had everything to be thankful for.

I didn't want to leave the old brown shoebox. But

once every ornament festooned the tree, I held the box gently.

It was empty now.

Empty.

Like my home.

Like my life.

What would I live for now? Who would I care for? I hadn't even realized how much of my time and attention had been taken up by caring for those dearest to me—first the children, then Philip as his health declined. And now... I was alone. Did my life still have purpose? Meaning?

This is part of everything.

Clarity washed over me in a flood. Of course my life had purpose, because my life was God's, and He had me here.

To pray.

To lift others up.

And to give thanks.

I inhabit the praises of My people. The still, small voice speaking to my heart was one I knew and loved, and I sank myself into the words. Yes. When I praised Him, I invited His presence.

And therefore, I was never alone.

Never.

I picked up the empty shoebox. The ornaments hung on the tree, each a memorial to a blessing God had given me, and I knew what I wanted to do with the box.

The day after tomorrow was Christmas Eve. I stacked my wrapped gifts for the children and grandchildren on the table. I'd have to mail them today if they were to arrive in time for Christmas. One by one, I lifted each gift out from under the tree and added them to the stack.

At last, only one box remained.

The old brown shoebox. I hesitated a moment, then picked it up and sank onto the sofa.

My one gift this year. For the first time in all my life, there was no one to exchange gifts with.

Only me. And God.

And this was my gift to Him.

I bowed over the shoebox, silent before Him. It wasn't Christmas yet, but the moment had come. Right now, before sending gifts to my loved ones, I wanted to exchange gifts with my Savior and King first. I slipped the lid off the box reverently, knowing exactly what I'd find inside. It had taken me the entire week, and now it was time.

Papers. Slips of paper. The box was full once more.

I unfolded one, then another, then a third. For an hour or more, I read. Every slip of paper detailed a specific blessing of my life. For every year I'd lived, God had done marvelous things. I'd searched through old journals and letters as well as my memory in writing these, but reading them all together proved an experience.

Had I *ever* truly realized how much I had to be grateful for?

When the children were young, I remembered being impatient. Wishing they'd grow up faster. Grudging the hours I'd had to spend feeding, tending, cleaning, and training them and wondering if I'd ever have time or energy for my own interests.

That was part of everything, and now I was truly thankful. What did my own interests matter in light of the kingdom work God had called me to in my family?

Philip. I'd never know, perhaps, all the reasons why

God had taken him and left me. But that was part of everything. And I was dimly becoming aware that, with Philip at my side, I would never have truly been able to be thankful in *everything*. Because he'd always been there, always the optimistic one, always the first to give thanks when the stove gave out, when he hit his thumb with a hammer, when the corn harvest was too small, when we'd grieved our stillborn Mary.

But now—*I* was the one who had to give thanks. I didn't have his optimism pouring into my ears. I couldn't lean on him any longer.

It was only me.

Me and God.

And God was enough.

No, more than that: God was everything.

And I could finally thank Him.

The words didn't want to leave my tongue. But, in the strength of His Spirit, I lifted up my voice. "Thank You, Yahweh, for taking Philip. Thank You for my loneliness. I receive all this as a gift from Your hand, for Your glory. Make me truly thankful, and may I rejoice in You in this. My gift to You." Tears streamed, landing like shimmering pearls upon my knuckles, but my lips curved into a smile. There was peace within, and I couldn't explain it.

"Thank You for that," I whispered. "Your precious gift to me."

At that moment, a firm knock sounded at the door, and then it cracked open. The sweetest familiar voice—no, two—no, three! all three of my very favorites in this world!—echoed through the hall, setting my heart bounding with unexpected joy as the biggest smile flew to my face.

"Mama? Are you crying over that old shoebox?"

117

EVERYTHING
BY REBEKAH A. MORRIS

WAS IT MY fault? Had I said the wrong things? Could I have said something different or in a different way? Maybe I had been too firm, too hard.

Burying my face in my pillow I sobbed out the stress and fear. I cried tears of frustration and sorrow. Why had this happened to me? Why had God put me in charge?

"Mindy?" The gentle voice held concern. "What's wrong, honey?" Dad's hand rested lightly on my head. "Come on, it can't be that bad, can it?"

"Y-yes!" I sobbed, still hiding my face. "I've ruined e-everything."

I felt the mattress sink as Dad sat down beside me, making me realize that he had climbed the old farmhouse steps in spite of his bad leg just to comfort me. That made me cry even harder. I was a failure as a daughter, a failure in my business, as well as a failure at being a good leader in the small group of graphic designers. Everything I did seemed to crumble and break apart in my hands.

Dad's hands, rough and hard from a lifetime of farm work, were gentle as they massaged my tight shoulders. "Tell me about it, honey."

"I've ruined everything, Daddy. Everything I try to do ends up failing."

"That lemon cake you made the other day sure didn't taste like it failed," Dad said softly.

"Well, everything big has failed." I gave a shuddering sob and turned my face to the wall.

"Tell me."

I knew Dad wouldn't leave until I talked, and I needed to tell someone. Perhaps it wouldn't hurt so much if my daddy were there to soothe the pain like he'd done so many times when I was young.

"I was at the graphic designers' meeting this afternoon," I began, thinking of the joy I had felt when I greeted my fellow designers as they came in. "The meeting started out well, but then one of them wanted to do something that would make more money. It made many of us uncomfortable. We didn't have anything in the by-laws about it though because we'd never had this happen before, but we had talked about it. The other leaders and I went into the other room and talked it over. We decided we didn't feel right about doing it. So we told the group no, and why. Well, the one girl got mad, and her friends got mad, and the next thing we knew half of our group got up and left, saying they didn't want to be a part of a group that was so narrowminded and...and stuck on themselves."

I felt the tears rolling down my cheeks again and soaking the pillow.

"What did the others do?" Daddy's voice was calm and steady like it was when one of the animals was having trouble giving birth or had become injured. Somehow it calmed me too.

"I didn't know what to do. Some of the other girls said they needed to be going and they left, and soon there were only a handful of us. One of the others asked if we'd done the right thing. We thought we had, but— Oh, Daddy, why do people cause so much hurt? We tried to be kind in explaining our stand, but they just got upset and wouldn't listen."

"Mindy, do you believe you made the right decision?" I thought a moment. Was I sure? "Yes."

"Then you don't have anything to do with how others react. All you can do is pray and leave everything up to God."

Leave everything up to God. Could I do that? Everything? Not just my worries about the graphic designers' group, but everything? Even my business problems? My fear that I was failing my daddy?

"Everything, Daddy?"

Daddy's hand smoothed my hair back from my face. "Well—"

I knew there had to be more that I was missing.

Daddy's voice was low. "The Bible says casting all our care on Him. Now what part of everything does *all* not cover, Mindy?"

Everything. All. They were the same. They covered each area of my life and then some, didn't they?

"Mindy?"

"It covers it all, Daddy."

"Yes, it does. We are to cast all—every single thing— on Him because He cares for us. Oh, Mindy girl, He cares so much for you! More than I ever could, and you know that I love you oh, so much!"

Rolling over, I sat up and flung my arms around Daddy's neck. "I know you do, Daddy! Thank you! It's hard to remember that God cares about the little things like the problem with the other designers, but since you care, I know He does too."

Daddy returned my hug. "Yes, He cares, but Mindy"—Daddy cupped my face in his worn hands—"you have to give everything to Him. Don't hold on to the least bit of it. He wants it all."

I nodded. "Thank you!" I couldn't say anything else right then.

With a tender smile, Daddy kissed my forehead and then rose. "I'm going to make some chicken noodle soup. Do you want to make some rolls to go with it?"

"Yes. I'll be there in a few minutes."

He nodded and left the room. I could hear him slowly making his way down the narrow farmhouse stairs. If my daddy on earth loved me so much and cared about me enough that he was willing to suffer pain to come up to my room to comfort me, how much more did my Heavenly Father love and care for me? The thought made me drop to my knees where I poured out everything that was bothering me and added, "Thank You for caring for me, and for giving me a Daddy who could show me such a wonderful picture of how much You love me!"

Then I rose, washed my face, and went down to make Daddy's favorite dinner rolls. And maybe I'd make him an apple crisp too.

EVERYTHING
BY A.F. KOPP

Tuckerton, Iowa
November 1864

EVERYTHING CHANGED AFTER the telegram. It's funny how when things change so quickly, it doesn't seem real. *It doesn't feel real*, I thought, staring at the mirror on the wall. The mirror distorted my image, but I could still see the red eyes and frazzled hair. Was it possible to age ten years in one day? The place above my heart felt even more empty as the ghost of my necklace taunted me of its absence. Why did I have to give it to him before he left? The necklace my dear sister bought for me was gone along with *him*.

My Lincoln. Gone.

He was everything I had left here. He and Bernie. He was the reason I stayed behind in the middle of cornfields in Iowa, instead of going back to the city with Mother, Father, and Chrissy. But I made the decision to stay—at the time it seemed the best decision. We married and soon enough little Bernie came along, and it was the three of us in Link's homestead. It was the life we built together. But now everything had changed.

Quickly, I tamed a few wisps of my hair, making myself more presentable before heading back downstairs. Bernie was probably wondering what was going on to make his mother rush upstairs for privacy. Descending the steps, I saw Papa Beckett, Lincoln's father, bouncing Bernie on his knee, singing a song into his ear. A bittersweet smile crept onto my lips, remembering Link doing the same to our son. Placing a hand above my heart, I let out a breath as if it would ease the pain. How I missed him, more than ever now.

Papa Beckett looked up, spotting me waiting at the entry of the dining room, where the telegram was placed precariously close to Bernie. Though he wasn't the best at reading yet, I didn't want him to know his father wasn't coming home from the war. I didn't want him to know yet.

"Maisie," Papa Beckett started but paused as tears glazed over his eyes. He had moved into our homestead when Lincoln went away to war to help keep the farm up. Papa Beckett wasn't too far along in age, but it was his back that kept him from the war and almost from the fields. He was just determined, much like his son, so nothing—not even his bad back—could stop him from what he was raised to do—farm good land.

"Papa, I know," was all I could get out as I took Bernie from my father-in-law's arms. Bernie buried his face into my neck, yawning quietly. My heart tugged in my chest. Though Link wasn't returning to Bernie and me, I could still be there for my son. I was everything he had left. "I'll be back. Bernie needs to sleep."

I carried my son upstairs, humming some unknown melody to him as his breathing got steadier and steadier. Bernie was an easy child, from what I'd gathered from my friends. My dear neighbor Rebecka Rickman told me how her oldest and youngest were vastly different in demeanor and ease of discipline. Henry Jr. was fussy, never slept, and had her chasing after him until he turned five—which was only a month ago. Bernie and Henry Jr. were about the same age and were quickly friends, though they had vastly different personalities.

I placed Bernie on the trundle bed beside my and Link's bed, plopping down on the mattress beside him. Pushing the thought of Lincoln out of my head, I brushed a strand of my son's hair out of his face. "My dearest boy," I whispered softly as his eyes fluttered with slumber. I kept stroking his hair and whispering sweet nothings to him until he drifted off to sleep.

I lay beside him on the small trundle bed as suddenly all my emotions crashed inside me like a wave against rocks on the shore. My breath hitched with a sob as my body was wracked with pain.

I'd never see my Link again.

Sitting up, I took in the room. It was bare besides the wardrobe and mirror. No pictures—we couldn't afford photographs or paintings. No plants, no silver dishes, nothing. If I had stayed with Mother and Father in Chicago, I'd have everything. My lessons for piano, painting, and stitching. Money to afford decor and nice clothing and entertainment—I hadn't seen the opera in years.

If I had just listened to my parents, I wouldn't be here in Tuckerton, Iowa mourning the loss of my everything. Maybe Mother and Father were right and I shouldn't have married him.

I began to feel self-pity rise in me, but one look over at my sleeping son beside me sent a new strength and determination rushing through my body. I couldn't give up. I couldn't regret it all. I had *him*.

And Bernie needed me.

Sometimes losing everything helps you see what you haven't lost. I haven't lost Bernie or Papa Beckett or the farm—yet, anyway. I knew that whatever I decided to do with the farm would need a lot of work. Link never finished his upgrades or additions before heading off to war. I could still feel his hands on my face as he promised me he'd be back so that we'd finally fix the house up to fit the twenty kids and many cats I'd adopt. He hated cats but loved me enough to promise me loads full.

Wiping tears from my cheeks, I walked down to where Papa Beckett still sat at the dining table. He barely looked up as I passed him, entering the kitchen to make some coffee.

Setting the water on the woodstove, I started to grind the beans, but felt extremely weak and began having a hard time handling the grinder.

"Woah, there," my father-in-law's voice whispered in my ear as I started shaking from tears. He wrapped his strong arms around me, hushing and holding me. Grounding me. Then it hit me that he was grieving, too. "I got you, little Maisie."

"It's so wrong," I cried out, holding onto my father-in-law tightly as if he was the lifeline keeping me together. "He was so perfect and wonderful. Link won't be here to see Bernie grow, t-to see him married or anything. And I lost my world. He was the whole reason I came here—stayed here. I gave up *everything* to be with him."

"I know, Maisie." Papa Beckett's voice was muffled against my shoulder as he sniffed, taking a shaky inhale. "But everything—" He choked on his words, pausing to recover himself. "Everything happens for a reason. God sees, Margarette. God sees it all."

My breath hitched. How could I have forgotten about

God? The God Who sees? The God Who created all things? The God Who knew everything?

My face contorted as realization hit me of God's realness. "Oh, Jesus, help me." I sank to the floor in sobs as I struggled to come to terms with God letting it happen to Link, but also with how I had to let him go. He was with Jesus now, rejoicing with the Father. But I was here with his earthly father, broken and grieving.

My chest felt stuck—tight. I couldn't control anything. I couldn't *change* anything. I had to move forward, but it was all so overwhelming. Everything shifted and changed now that he was gone. But I knew that the God who saw everything from the foundations of the earth was beside me. His peace was waiting for me. I knew He could fill the ever-gaping hole that grew in my heart, but I just had to let Him in. I had to let Him change everything I knew about life and no longer take things into my own hands. I had to learn to trust Him.

Wiping the tears from my eyes, I let my hands fall to my lap, exhaustion setting in. I looked up at Papa Beckett, who leaned against the counter, hand covering his salt-and-pepper beard as his mouth moved silently in prayer. He opened his fierce dark eyes, looking down at me with an intensity and intention that startled me.

"What do we do?" I asked, crossing my arms over my chest as I shivered out of nowhere. "With the farm? With everything?" I trailed off, pursing my lips.

"Time will tell, Margarette," Papa Beckett responded, letting out a huge breath he had been holding, helping me up from the floor. "But before we can do anything, I think it's best that we do mourn properly. I'll be out in the fields if you need me."

A small, forced smile played on my lips as he kissed

my forehead, grabbing his coat from the rack by the door. With a rush of cold wind, he was gone, exploring his favorite wildflower patch.

Now that he was gone, it was only me and my feelings and God. Something that was so very uncomfortable, but so much needed. I laughed aloud. I had lived life as if I only got the blue skies but neglected the thought of facing the wrestles with God. Besides the wrestle of transitioning from my wealthy upbringing to having almost nothing besides love, I had life easy. It was simple. But now things were not so. Link had been my crutch. Papa Beckett had been my crutch. Bernie, too.

So, now, in the kitchen with no one around, I had reached my lowest. But sometimes you have to lose everything to lose yourself. To lose your self-satisfying and sufficiency. Would I understand all of it now? *No*, I scoffed to myself. I didn't understand any of it now. But I knew that maybe years in the future I'd be able to look back and see everything that God had done through this moment. Through losing it all. Through the wrestle. Somehow, through losing everything, I gained something more important—faith.

The End

EVERYTHING
BY HANNAH E. GRIGGS

THE LATE AFTERNOON sun filtered through the countless skyscrapers, somehow managing to find its way through to the pavement below that swarmed with cars.

Inside one of the many yellow taxis on the highway, music filled every corner as the well-blended voices of a men's quartet came through the speakers. "This is my story, this is my song, praising my Savior, all the day long."

The businessman in the back seat of the taxi frowned. "Would you mind turning off that noise?" he called up to the driver.

With a smile, Frank, the taxi driver, pushed the button to turn off the radio. "Is that better?" He looked in the rearview mirror at his passenger.

"Much better. I heard enough of those songs when I was a kid to last me a lifetime."

Frank steered the taxi onto the highway. "Say, sir, if you died tonight, do you know where you would go, Heaven or Hell?"

"On second thought, maybe that radio station wasn't so bad after all," the passenger retorted.

Frank looked at the clock on the dash and grinned.

His favorite preacher was just coming on. He turned the radio on and adjusted the volume to where his passenger couldn't miss it. He smiled to himself as he looked out over the sparkling waters of Lake Michigan. This man was sure to hear a good message during the rest of his taxi ride, and since it was just after five o'clock, it could take a while in the bumper-to-bumper work traffic.

"Frank, are you going to be able to come to the Wednesday evening service this week?" the high-pitched female voice asked through the phone.

Frank kept back a sigh, knowing his older sister Tammy wouldn't be happy with his answer. "No, I have to work." He rested his elbow on his kitchen table and awaited his sister's lecture that was as predictable as the wind that blew down from the lake across the Windy City.

"You really ought to be there, Frank. We're having an evangelist speak about ways to get involved in ministry. I think it would be good for you to hear."

This time, Frank didn't bother to hold back his sigh. "Tammy, how many times do I have to tell you my taxi driving is my ministry?"

"I know that's what you say. It makes for a handy excuse. But does giving out a tract to one of your customers now and then count as a ministry? You need to be more involved in the church. There's a vacant Sunday School class right now. We need a teacher for the four- to eight-year-olds."

Frank laughed. "Me teaching that age? I don't know the first thing about teaching kids. About all I know to do for them is give them candy, and I know their parents would just love that right before service."

"Well, you could learn. I'd take it, but I already have my own class."

"I'm sorry, Tammy. But I just don't think God is leading me in that direction. I'd like to come tomorrow night, but I can't make it." Frank politely ended the call and thumped his phone down on the table.

I wish Tammy wasn't always harping at me about needing to be involved in ministry. Why can't she understand that my taxi job is my ministry? I get to witness to people who would never set foot inside a church, like that businessman the other day and those atheist college students this morning. Well, at least I know this is what God wants me to do. It would be nice if Tammy understood and was sympathetic, but that's not really what matters. What matters is doing exactly what God wants me to do, and I know this is what He has called me to do.

Wednesday night, Frank pulled up to the curb on a dark street to pick up a customer. He was in a rough part of the city known for violent crime. Already he had seen three police cars racing by, their lights flashing. The sight of his customer didn't ease his concerns any.

He looks the gangster type, Frank mused.

His passenger, a young man, his face mostly concealed by a hoodie, slouched up to the car, got in the backseat, and gave Frank the address of his destination.

Frank turned the radio on and drove down the street. This would be a lengthy trip all the way across the city. As he drove, he prayed for his passenger and for God to give him wisdom to know when to start speaking and what to say. *I don't want to say anything that gets me stabbed in the back unless this is God's time and way for me to go.*

"My grandma used to sing that song," the young man said from the back seat.

Frank turned the radio down a bit. "Is that so? Did

she go to church?"

"Yeah, she did. She took me and my sister a time or two when we were kids."

"Do you have a church you attend now?"

The young man laughed loudly. "Man, nobody would want me stepping foot in their church."

"I would," Frank said quietly. By the streetlights illuminating the inside of the car, he saw the young man stare at him, but before he could say anything, Frank asked one of his usual questions he always had ready to use. "If you died tonight, would you go to Heaven or Hell?"

The passenger shifted uncomfortably on the seat, fidgeting with his seatbelt and tapping on the car door beside him. "Man, I don't think God would let me into Heaven. I've done too many bad things. So I guess—I guess I'd get sent to the other place."

"Is that what you want?" Frank asked.

"No. But I can't make myself good enough for Heaven. So I just keep doing whatever I want and don't think about dying." He paused. "But that doesn't always work. A buddy of mine was killed the other day, and it got me thinking again about what will happen when I die."

That explains why he's so open. Death often gets people thinking about their eternal destiny. Aloud, Frank said, "What's your name, son?"

"Darren."

"Well, Darren, you said you can't make yourself good enough to go to Heaven. Neither can I, but I know that's where I'm going when I die."

In the rearview mirror, Frank saw perplexity on Darren's face. "How do you know?"

"I know because I'm trusting Jesus to take me there. Do you know who Jesus is?"

"I've heard of Him. But I don't guess I know who He is."

In simple terms, Frank explained that Jesus was the Son of God who had come to earth to die on the cross to pay the penalty for the sins of every man, woman, and child who had ever lived. He also told about how Jesus conquered death by rising from the dead on the third day and how if Darren chose to surrender his life to Jesus, he could be assured that he too would go to Heaven when he died.

All too soon, they reached Darren's destination, and he opened the door to climb out.

"Thanks, man, for all you said. You've given me a lot to think about."

Frank pulled a book and some pamphlets out of the compartment of his door. "Here are some things for you to read. They go into more detail than what I said."

Darren took the literature with a big grin. "I sure appreciate it. And I'll read it."

As Frank drove away, heading home to his apartment, he couldn't help thinking, *And Tammy thinks I don't have a ministry. She thought I needed to be at church tonight to learn about how I can work for God. I know I don't know everything there is to know about working for God, but I also know God had me here for a reason tonight. If I'd been in church, I wouldn't have met Darren during this time when he was open to hearing the Gospel.*

A few days later, Frank pulled up outside an apartment complex that had grown quite familiar to him over the last few months.

A young woman with her two children came down

the outside stairs. One was a boy of around seven. The other was a toddler. Frank already had the booster seat ready for the chubby-cheeked little girl who climbed in.

"Hi, Mistah Fwank." She greeted him with a big smile.

"Hi, Cassie." Frank returned her smile and gave her older brother one that was just as big. "How's Benny today?"

The boy's smile was faint. "I'm okay, Mr. Frank."

The children's mother had gotten Cassie buckled in, and she now settled into her seat.

"Good afternoon, Candace," Frank greeted her.

"Hi." She gave him a weary smile.

The first part of the drive, only the radio could be heard in the car. But as they crossed one of the many drawbridges and turned and drove along the gleaming waters of Lake Michigan, Benny and Cassie cried eagerly about the boats they saw.

"Look at the sailboat!" Benny exclaimed. "I wish we had one of those."

"I can think of a lot of things we need worse than a sailboat," Candace said. "Like a car."

Frank knew she was referring to the many trips they made with him to all of Benny's doctor's appointments. Benny was battling cancer, and the doctor had recommended that they use a taxi to go to the doctor's appointments since there would be less chance of him catching something than on the L, the crowded overhead train.

Frank had gotten fairly-well acquainted with Candace and knew that she was interested in the Gospel. He also could tell when she was willing to hear it and discuss it with him, but today wasn't one of those days.

When they were nearing the hospital, Benny asked, "Mr. Frank, do you have any of those little comics? I like reading them while I have my treatment."

Frank knew exactly what Benny was asking for. He often gave the boy comic tracts. "When we get parked, I'll see if I have any new ones. I think you've read a lot of them."

They reached the entrance to the hospital, and Frank pulled up under the awning to let his passengers off at the door. While Candace unbuckled Cassie, Frank looked through his box of tracts. Benny leaned over the seat, looking too.

"Here's a new one I just got." Frank pulled out a little pamphlet with a picture of a dog on the cover. "I think you'll enjoy the story."

Benny took the tract with a "Thank you."

Frank handed a lollipop to Cassie. "Here you go, little lady. I'd give you one too, Benny, but I know the doctor and your mom don't want you having a lot of sugar right now."

"It's okay," Benny said. "I'd rather read."

"Come on, kids." Candace took Cassie's hand. "We'll see you when we get done, Frank."

"All right." Before driving off, Frank looked down at the next address he was going to: a hotel in the downtown area. The destination was the Willis Tower. *Tourists, I'm sure,* he mused, putting his car in gear and slowly pulling away from the curb. *No doubt they're wanting a good view of Chicago and to see if they get scared out of their wits on the glass floor.* He chuckled, remembering the time he and Tammy had gone with friends when they were in their teens, how Tammy had frozen out on the glass floor, more than thirteen hundred feet above the city, and had to be helped off.

He soon found his guess about his customers was right. The family was passing through Chicago on a trip and had wanted to see some of the sights. Frank was also pleasantly surprised to find out they were a Christian family.

He visited briefly with them and pointed out some sites that would be of interest to them, the historic Moody Church being one of them. But mostly, Frank spent his time watching out for the heavy traffic of the downtown area as he drove down the streets shaded by the overhead train. He also enjoyed listening to the two girls in the backseat *ooh*ing and *aah*ing over the sights.

"I never saw so many taxis in my life," the older of the two girls said.

"And so many people," the younger one said. "Oh, look! I recognize that orange modern art sculpture!"

"You must not be from a big city," Frank said to the dad.

He grinned. "No, we're from a very small town. So this is quite an adventure for us."

Frank flipped on his turn signal and turned onto Wacker Drive when the traffic light changed to a green arrow. "It really will be an adventure on the Skydeck. Hope you guys enjoy it!"

After dropping his passengers off at their destination, Frank drove to pick up another downtown customer, who was on his way to the Pacific Garden Mission where he would be speaking that night.

When the customer had been dropped off, he returned to the hospital. It should be about time to pick up Candace and her children. Since learning about their situation and how tight their finances were, Frank always gave them a discount on their fare, another way he could minister to this needy family.

That evening Frank saw another familiar address he would be visiting: a local college. One of the students must be needing a ride somewhere.

When he pulled up outside one of the dorms, Frank

recognized Jeremy, a young student who was a Christian and sometimes visited his church.

Jeremy climbed in the back seat and deposited his backpack on the seat beside him.

"How's school going?" Frank asked, driving down the street.

"Most of my classes are going okay."

"But not all of them?"

Jeremy sighed. "There's this one professor who knows I'm a Christian, and he does everything he can to make fun of me and try to change my beliefs."

"Is he succeeding?" The traffic light turned green, and Frank proceeded through the intersection after making sure there were no pedestrians trying to cross the street at the last minute.

"I don't know. Today he brought up the resurrection of Jesus Christ, and he had some arguments I never heard before."

Frank smiled in the dark. He could imagine what scenarios a skeptical professor might have brought up. "What did he say? I might have some answers for you."

"He said that maybe Jesus wasn't really dead and was able to get out of the grave. Or maybe the disciples went to the wrong tomb."

"Those are both arguments I've heard, and I've also heard some answers for them. Let's look first at the argument that Jesus wasn't really dead. First, it was the death penalty for a Roman soldier if one of his prisoners got off a cross alive. So they would have been experts at telling if a person had just fainted or was really dead. And if Jesus hadn't been dead, do you think after three days with no food or water and no medical care that He would have been able to roll away the stone that weighed several tons, overpower the Roman soldiers who stood guard, and escape from them?"

"That really doesn't seem likely," Jeremy admitted. "I'm surprised my professor didn't think of that."

"Well, he doesn't want the resurrection to be true, so he wouldn't be looking for proofs that it happened. Now for the idea that the disciples may have gone to the wrong tomb. If they went to the wrong tomb, so did everyone else. All the Jewish leaders would have had to do was produce the body from the right tomb, and that would have been the end of it. The right tomb was sealed with a Roman seal, but a wrong tomb wouldn't have had that."

As Frank finished giving his explanation, they pulled up at Jeremy's destination. The young man leaned forward before getting out of the taxi. "Thanks, Frank. You've helped me more than you realize. It strengthens my faith to have proof for what I believe, and you've given it to me."

After Jeremy had gotten out and closed the car door, Frank bowed his head and thanked God for this opportunity. God had used him to help strengthen a younger brother's faith in Christ.

Frank pulled up his profile on the website and looked at it with a groan. *There are even more bad reviews than last time I checked. Well, I guess anyone who rides with me will know what they're getting into. Some of these reviews are downright filthy and others are rude. Oh well, God never said working for Him would be easy. And this isn't anything compared with how other Christians have suffered for Him. If all I get are a few one-star reviews and people griping in the comments about how I share my faith with them, I'll be getting off easy.* Frank's phone rang and he looked down at the screen. *Tammy.*

I wonder what she wants this time.

"Hello."

"Hi Frank. Can you come over for dinner tonight? Or are you working?"

"No, I'm not working, so I can come over." He really didn't want to, but he knew he couldn't ignore his sister, even though she always wanted to talk about the same thing.

"All right. We'll be looking for you around five-thirty."

Trained to always arrive on time to pick up customers, Frank pulled into the driveway of his sister's house at exactly five-thirty. The door was opened by his niece Lexi, a pretty girl of about sixteen. She was quickly joined by the eight-year-old twins, Logan and Lucas.

The boys rushed their uncle off to the family room to show him their latest invention with building blocks. Presently, their mom entered the room and announced that dinner was ready. The family gathered at the table, and Tammy's husband Shawn asked the blessing. All through dinner, Frank waited for Tammy to bring up another idea of how he could get involved in some sort of ministry. When she didn't, he decided that maybe she didn't want to discuss it in front of the children.

Finally, the twins had gone back to the den to keep building their model of Wrigley Field, and Lexi had gone to her room to finish her homework.

Tammy folded her hands on the table, and Frank knew what was coming.

"How's your ministry going, Frank?"

Frank blinked. Was she genuinely asking, or was she being sarcastic? "Fine," he answered shortly.

Tammy looked over at Shawn, and he spoke up. "Tammy and I had a little excitement a couple nights ago. We were going to visit one of Tammy's Sunday School students who doesn't live in the best part of town, and as we were leaving there, we had a flat tire."

"Were you able to get it fixed all right?" Frank asked.

"That's where the excitement began." As Tammy spoke, her voice rose higher in pitch and took on her storytelling tone she had perfected after many years of teaching the junior Sunday School class. "The alley we were in when it happened was dark, deserted, exactly the kind of place you hear about people getting knifed in the back. All we wanted to do was get the tire changed and get out of there as quickly as possible. But we found out that was not to be the case when we heard approaching footsteps. Shawn had gotten out the jack and the donut and was trying to get the flat tire off when I saw this man step out of the shadows. He was dressed in dark clothes, and I knew he must belong to one of the gangs that roam that area. I thought for sure he had come to rob us or even worse, but to my surprise, he offered to help Shawn change the tire."

"I didn't want to accept his help," Shawn put in. "But I was also afraid that if I said no, he might get upset and turn violent or something. And if he was right there helping me change the tire, I could at least keep an eye on him. So I let him help me."

"I was praying the whole time, not knowing if he was a thug or just someone who looked rough on the outside. I just knew when the tire was changed, he was going to steal our car and leave us stranded there in that dark alley. But when he and Shawn were done, and Shawn had handed him a Gospel tract, would you believe it? He said he already had one of those. He pulled it out of his pocket and showed it to us."

Frank couldn't keep back a grin. He was having his

suspicions of who this Good Samaritan had been.

Tammy continued with her story. "He said that he had been given that tract and a book a few weeks before and now he is a child of God. He also said that before he became a Christian, if he'd seen us stranded there, he'd have robbed us. But he said now Jesus is in control of his life, and that's not something Jesus would do."

Here, Shawn took up the story. "In fact, a couple of his buddies showed up, but because their friend was there helping us, they were polite and respectful. They even took a couple of tracts before leaving."

Tammy reached out a hand and rested it on Frank's arm. "Frank, we asked the young man where he got the tract and book, and he said it was from a taxi driver. Was that you?"

"Was the young man's name Darren?" Frank asked.

Shawn and Tammy looked at each other. "It was," Tammy answered quietly. "Oh, Frank, I've been so wrong in the way I thought you weren't doing much for God. You do have a ministry. And it's just as important as Shawn being an assistant pastor or me being a Sunday School teacher."

Shawn cleared his throat. "Yes, since we met Darren, we've been doing a lot of thinking. We've realized that everything God calls a Christian to do, whether it be pastor, doctor, foreign missionary, or taxi driver, can be used to bring glory to God and grow His Kingdom."

Frank could hardly believe the words he was hearing. His sister and brother-in-law finally supported him in what he did? God had brought Darren across their path to show them that each and every calling is important. He smiled at Tammy. "I'm glad God showed you this. And you want to hear something interesting? The night I met Darren was the Wednesday night you wanted me to go hear the evangelist speak about becoming involved in Christian ministry."

Tammy blushed. "You've known what it means to be involved in ministry more than we have. But now God has opened our eyes to the truth. And any time you need our help with any aspect of your ministry, we'll help you all we can."

Frank couldn't help noticing the young man and his girlfriend roll their eyes at each other as he asked them the question, "If you died tonight and God asked you why He should let you into Heaven, what would you say?"

The girlfriend's answer was sarcastic, and the young man used language Frank would never have repeated. They ended up asking to get out right there, saying they didn't want to give their money to a religious nut. "We'll get another taxi," the young man said. "We can wait a little longer to get to the Bean."

As Frank pulled away from the curb and resumed his drive down the busy street, past numerous skyscrapers, he prayed for the young people, that they would see their need to be saved before it was too late.

He also added on to his prayer, *Thank you for changing Tammy and Shawn's heart. And thank You that even though I'm not what most people would consider someone in full-time Christian ministry that I can still work for You. Thank You that everything, if done for Your glory, can further Your Kingdom and be used to minister to others.*

EVERYTHING

BY AUTUMN NICOLE

THE STEADY RHYTHM of the heart monitor and the stark white walls of the hospital room gave Avaline a headache. She slouched in the hard chair and pressed her fingers to her temples, closing her eyes—but only for a brief moment. Determined to keep her faithful vigil, she returned her gaze to the still form on the bed. Her mother's face was as pale as the sheets she rested on.

Fresh tears pricking her eyes, Avaline rose from the chair and padded softly across the room. Sinking to her knees by the bed, she clasped her mother's chilled hand between both of her own.

"Mama," she whispered, choking back emotion. "Please don't leave me. I need you here."

She lowered her head to the bed as tears spilled down her cheeks. Exhaustion tugged her toward dreamland, and she made no effort to resist. All she wanted was to fall asleep and wake up from this dreadful nightmare.

A soft knock at the door pulled Avaline awake. With a moan, she lifted her head from the bed she still knelt beside and ran a hand through her tangled curls.

The door opened and a nurse, with her hair pulled back in a French braid, stepped in, a sweet smile reaching to her compassionate blue eyes. She clasped a clipboard to her chest, and a stethoscope hung loosely around her neck.

She stepped to the side of the bed and rested a hand on Avaline's shoulder. "Honey, why don't you go get something to drink from the cafeteria? Tell them Gracie sent you. You look exhausted."

Avaline shook her head. "No, thanks, I'll stay here." Her hand closed tighter around her mother's.

The nurse's hand on her shoulder didn't move. "Your mother will be in good hands. Go get some fresh air."

Avaline bit her lip and glanced at her mother again. Her face was so pale. All drained of color. The same raven-black curls Avaline had inherited clung to her forehead and seemed to be the only color left to her once vibrant face.

Swallowing hard, Avaline silently rose from her position and bent down to kiss her mother on the cheek. The nurse's hand never left her shoulder until she turned away. She grabbed her sparkly purple journal off the nightstand and after a moment of hesitation reached for her soft leather Bible too. She slipped from the room, closing the door softly behind her.

Hugging the books to her chest, Avaline wrapped her fuzzy gray cardigan closer around herself as she walked down the hospital hallways to the elevator. After receiving a special cup of cocoa from the cafeteria's cook, she found her way to the hospital doors and escaped to the icy February air that whipped her hair around her face.

An ambulance wailed in the distance. A lump choked

her throat, and she lifted a cardigan-covered hand to her mouth to hold back the emotion.

She found a small grassy area nearby and settled back against the trunk of a bare oak tree, pulling her knees up. She wrapped her hands tightly around the hot cocoa cup and took a small sip. She could feel it warming her insides all the way down. She shivered. After setting the cup beside her and settling it into a position where it wouldn't tip over, she opened her journal and balanced it on her knees. For a long moment she stared blankly out over the hospital parking lot, chewing on the end of her pen as she tried to form her scattered thoughts into words.

With a sigh, she put her pen to paper.

Everything is crumbling.

Her crooked handwriting was barely legible as she scrawled words quickly on the page. Her tears froze on her face as she wrote.

God, why is this happening to me? I already lost Daddy only three years ago. And then Reed left last year and now he won't respond to my texts—not even when I told him Mama was sick! God, are you going to take Mama away too? I don't think I could bear it. I know I can't bear it.

She pushed the hair away from her face and took another sip of cocoa. Her phone dinged in her pocket, but she ignored it.

My senior year was supposed to be spent visiting colleges, not hospitals. I should probably take an extra job to help pay for her medical bills. Reed sure won't offer any assistance. Between watching over Mama and working an extra job, I probably won't have time for school, even if they allow me to do all my work at home. I probably won't even be able to graduate this year.

She paused and swiped at her eyes with her sleeve. Maybe she was getting carried away with jumping to

145

conclusions, but she didn't care. Things couldn't get much worse than they already were.

Why even try? I should drop out of school. I'll work until Mama—no, I won't even say it. And then I'll have to somehow keep up with the mortgage payments for the house so I have a place to live. I'll somehow have to make it on my own. I'll have to work low-paying jobs because no one will want to hire someone who dropped out of school three months from graduating.

She took a deep breath and redirected her thoughts.

Why would God allow this to happen to me? Why would He take all of my family from me? Wasn't one loss enough? God, why would you do this to me? Don't you care? Must you take everything away from me?

I feel like everything is falling apart. It's like I'm trapped in a building that's caving in on top of me—and I'm all alone. God, I'm so scared. I feel lost and abandoned—like You don't even care anymore. God, why can't You just fix everything?!

Avaline slammed her journal shut and covered her face with her hands. Sobbing, she rested her elbows on her knees and dug her palms into her eyes to try to hold back the tears.

She slipped to the ground and curled into a ball at the base of the towering tree, pulling her cardigan tightly around her as the tears fell relentlessly. The cold air burned her throat as she sucked in sharp breaths between the sobs.

Lifting her eyes toward the clear blue sky, she tried to pray. "God, I know You love me. I really do. I've felt Your love. I know You are right here with me, and I know You care. Please help me truly believe it in my heart, not just know it in my head."

A cloud drifted lazily by. How long she lay there, she didn't know. But with sudden compulsion, she sat up quickly and reached for her Bible. Scooting back against the trunk of the tree, she let it fall open on her lap. The Psalms had always been comforting whenever she faced something hard. She turned a few pages, scanning for a heading to catch her eye.

Her gaze fell on Psalm 91. The heading was highlighted in pink, and smudged black ink was scrawled in every open space around the printed words. A smile tugged at her lips. She had forgotten this passage.

Lifting her gaze to the tree branches she began reciting from memory.

"He that dwelleth in the secret place of the most High shall abide under the shadow of the Almighty. I will say of the Lord, He is my refuge and my fortress: my God; in Him will I trust."

A tear froze on her cheek. *God, You are my refuge! A fortress that never crumbles.*

"Surely He shall deliver thee from the snare of the fowler, and from the noisome pestilence. He shall cover thee with His feathers, and under His wings shalt thou trust: His truth shall be thy shield and buckler. Thou shalt not be afraid for the terror by night; nor for the arrow that flieth by day; Nor for the pestilence that walketh in darkness; nor for the destruction that wasteth at noonday."

Though everything crumbles around me, Your wings are always safe. I have no reason to be afraid!

"A thousand shall fall at thy side, and ten thousand at thy right hand; but it shall not come nigh thee. Only with thine eyes shalt thou behold and see the reward of the wicked. Because thou hast made the Lord, which is my refuge, even the most High, thy habitation; There shall no evil befall thee, neither shall any plague come nigh thy dwelling. For he shall give his angels charge over thee, to keep thee in all thy ways. They shall

bear thee up in their hands, lest thou dash thy foot against a stone. Thou shalt tread upon the lion and adder: the young lion and the dragon shalt thou trample under feet."

God, how I so easily doubt Your love and protection.

"Because he hath set his love upon me, therefore will I deliver him: I will set him on high, because he hath known my name. He shall call upon me, and I will answer him: I will be with him in trouble; I will deliver him, and honor him. With long life will I satisfy him, and shew him my salvation."

Tears streamed down her face, but her heart felt full. A peace now rested all around her. She slumped back against the tree and sighed, allowing her eyes to fall shut. "Thank you, Jesus."

A bitter wind snapped her from her moment of peace. Collecting her books and mug, she turned her steps toward the hospital. As she walked through the doors and breathed in the smell of the waiting room, she felt a tug at her spirit to once again sink into despair. She made her way back through the halls, her feet dragging as she tried to keep a smile in her spirit.

The sound of a commotion and quick feet drew her attention. She turned to see several nurses running with a gurney. Hurrying to get out of the way, Avaline pushed herself back against the wall. It gave way behind her and she found herself stumbling into someone's room.

"I'm so sorry," she stuttered. "I didn't mean to—"

"Did you come to visit me?" The little girl in the bed pushed herself up on her pillows. The blanket fell from her chest, revealing a flowy dress patterned with butterflies. Her head was completely shaved, but her blue eyes sparkled with such life, Avaline thought she had never seen a more beautiful child.

Avaline shook her head. "I'm sorry, I didn't. I really should get back to my mom."

The girl's face fell. "Oh, okay."

Feeling sorry for her, Avaline smiled slightly. "I suppose I can stay for a few minutes." She slid her phone out of her pocket to check the time. The forgotten text message jumped out at her. It was from an unknown number, but she bit back a gasp as she read the first few words.

Hey sis!

With an angry glare, she shoved the phone back into her pocket. Reed? How dare he address her so cheerfully after fifteen months of total silence. She seethed.

"Are you okay?"

Avaline blinked quickly and lifted her eyes to the young girl, who was watching her with curious concern.

"Yes, I'm fine."

The little girl shook her head mischievously. "I can tell when people are lying."

"What?" Avaline lifted an eyebrow, caught off guard.

"You lied. Your eyes are all red, which means you've been crying, so you're not fine." She crossed her arms and shot her the look of an unimpressed mother.

Avaline pouted. "Fine, Little-Miss-Detective. Maybe I'm not fine. But I don't want to talk about it."

The girl shrugged. "Mommy always says if there's something I don't want to talk about, it's probably because I need to talk about it."

Avaline smirked. "Sounds like something my mom would say."

The girl smiled sweetly. "Come sit with me. I like to ask questions."

Avaline reluctantly sat down on the side of the bed.

"Okay."

The girl adjusted the blanket over her lap and leaned forward, holding out a hand. "My name is Layla, and I'm nine. I have cancer, and I heard the doctors whispering when they thought I was asleep that I'm going to die next week."

Avaline stared at her for a moment, unsure of how to respond. She hesitantly reached out and shook her hand.

Layla continued without pausing for a breath. "What's your name? How old are you? Why are you here?"

Avaline grimaced. "My name is Avaline and I'm—"

"Avaline! What a pretty name! Do people call you Avy?" Layla's eyes sparkled.

Avaline smiled sadly. "My brother used to call me that."

"He doesn't call you that anymore?"

"I haven't seen him in over a year."

"Oh. Why?"

"You sure are nosy." Avaline bit her lip yet found herself readily providing Layla with more details. "He got mad at Mama and ran away. He wanted to be on his own."

"I'm sorry." Layla's face displayed genuine concern and sympathy. "I'll bet he was pretty cool. I always wanted an older brother. Instead, I have three younger ones." She made a face.

Avaline chuckled. "I'm sure when they are all grown up, they'll feel like older brothers—especially if they get taller than you."

Layla laughed. "No, I'll always be taller than them! I'll be up with Jesus and be able to always look down on them."

Avaline blinked, completely at a loss for what to say.

"You haven't answered my other questions yet. How old are you?"

"Eighteen."

Layla sighed happily. "I'm pretty positive I'll be eighteen in Heaven. I can't wait." She closed her eyes dreamily for a second, then they popped back open, still full of life. "Why are you here at the hospital? You don't look sick. Of course, I didn't look sick for a long time too."

"I'm not sick. Mama is." Avaline looked away.

A small hand slipped into hers, and when her gaze returned to the blue eyes, they were brimming with tears.

"Does she have cancer?" Layla asked quietly.

"I don't know. They can't figure out what's wrong with her. We've visited five different hospitals. Nobody can give us answers. But they don't think she'll last much longer."

Layla patted her knee. "It's hard, isn't it?"

Avaline nodded.

"My grandpa was really sick last year. But Jesus healed him when He took him home."

Avaline brushed her hair out of her eyes. "I'm glad he's better."

"Oh, yes!" All sadness was gone from Layla's bright face. "I know he's so happy in Heaven, and I can't wait to see him again."

Confusion furrowed Avaline's brow. "He—died?"

Layla nodded. "I said that already. Jesus took him home."

"But you said Jesus healed him!"

Now it was Layla's turn to look confused. "Of course! No one is sick in Heaven!"

Avaline looked away, her gaze wandering to a vase of roses on the bedside table. "Who gave those to you?"

"Daddy." Layla's eyes glazed over dreamily. "For Valentine's Day. He said I'm the prettiest girl in the world. Besides Mommy, of course," she added as an afterthought.

Avaline offered a sad smile.

"Did anyone give you flowers for Valentine's Day? Do you have a boyfriend?" Layla continued without pause as Avaline shook her head. "No flowers? Your daddy didn't even get you any? My daddy says he'll get me flowers every year until there's someone else to get them for me. And don't tell him I said so, but I think this will be the last year Daddy gets them for me. Someone else is getting me flowers next year." Layla's eyes twinkled mischievously.

"Oh?" A genuine grin spread across Avaline's face. "Who?"

"Jesus!" Layla's entire face glowed.

Avaline's grin wobbled. "Layla, how can you be so happy?"

Layla smiled sweetly. "Because Jesus lives inside me!"

"If I'm being honest, I'd tell you Jesus lives inside of me too, but I'm not very happy."

Layla leaned forward and placed both her hands on Avaline's leg. "I guess you haven't learned yet how to let Jesus truly live inside of you. It took me a long time too."

Avaline raised an eyebrow. "What do you mean?"

"Daddy likes to make analogies. He once told me this one. Have you ever ridden on your daddy's shoulders when you were little?"

Avaline smiled with sweet remembrance. "All the time."

Layla's smile matched her own. "Were you ever afraid?"

Avaline's brow furrowed. "No."

"Why? You sure were awfully high up."

Avaline shrugged. "Yeah, but I knew my dad wouldn't drop me. I trusted him."

Layla's blue eyes twinkled as she pointed a finger at Avaline. "Exactly. You trusted him. Even in what would normally be a scary place, you weren't scared because you trusted who held you."

Avaline nodded, deep in thought.

"Avy." Layla's voice brought Avaline's gaze back to her face. Her expression was somber and serious as she pondered her words before she spoke. "There's a verse somewhere in the Psalms that talks about those who live in the shadow of the Almighty. About God being our refuge and our fortress. We trust Him because He covers us with His wings.

"You see, the feathers on a bird's wings are designed in such a way that the water rolls off them. If we are under God's feathers, the water won't touch us. It doesn't mean it isn't raining—sometimes it's pouring! Even hailing! But we are safe, because God holds us. Do you understand what I'm saying?"

"Mm-hmm. You've given me a lot to think about. And I think you're pretty wise for a nine-year-old." Avaline smiled through her tears.

Layla laughed. "That's what Mommy says too."

"So that's why you're happy? Because you trust Jesus?"

"That's part of the reason." She looked earnestly into Avaline's eyes. "Avy, my daddy always likes to remind me I can't be happy by myself. I'm happy because Jesus is happy in my heart. He makes me happy. And because I know even if everything crumbles on top of me, even if it's hailing boulders in my life"—here she grinned—"Jesus is my refuge. I'm safe with Him. Even—" She reached out and squeezed Avaline's hand. "Even if it means death."

Avaline's voice choked with emotion. She squeezed Layla's hands with her own. "How did you learn so much?"

Layla grinned. "My parents, mostly. They've read the

Bible to me every night ever since I was born. At least that's what they told me, though I don't remember those first few years. I read it a lot now too." She reached under her pillow and pulled out a Bible covered with pink leather. "The pages are all curled and worn now. Several of them I can't even read because my tears washed away all the ink." Her face glowed. "But Jesus' words bring me comfort. And they teach me more about Him every day."

Avaline nodded. "I should read my Bible more. I do have Psalm 91 memorized. It often comforts me. But I guess at my age you have a hard time translating comfort and safety to happiness."

Layla looked at her curiously. "I don't think I know what you mean."

"For you, because you trust Jesus so much, you're not the least bit afraid; you're so happy. For me, even if I fully trust Jesus, I don't think I can be as cheerful as you."

Layla fingered the sleeve of her dress. "I didn't say I wasn't scared. It's good you weren't here yesterday. I was a wreck." Layla looked down sheepishly. "I didn't used to be this happy." She looked up with a wide smile on her lips. "But over the years, through lots of tears and prayers, Jesus has helped me be happy. Like I said, I'm happy because Jesus is happy through me."

Avaline rubbed a finger along the corner of Layla's Bible, pondering.

Layla laid a hand on top of hers. "Keep praying and reading. The more time you spend with Jesus, the more you will trust Him and the happier you'll be! But it takes time. Don't give up."

Avaline nodded. "Thank you, Layla. I'll do that."

Layla smiled. "You're welcome, Avy!" Her face suddenly paled and a look of pain stole the smile away.

Avaline started. "Layla! Are you okay?"

Layla nodded weakly and fell back against the pillows. Her voice was small. "I'll be okay. It will pass soon."

Avaline slipped off the bed and wrapped the girl's small hand in her own. "Should I call your mom? Where is she?"

Layla's eyes closed. "She went to pick up my brothers from Grandma's. She'll be back soon. It's okay. I need to sleep for a while. I'll be fine." She smiled slightly, despite the grimace of pain. "You'd make a good nurse."

"I don't know about that." Avaline smiled.

"Goodbye, Avy." Layla gave her hand a squeeze.

"Thank you for helping me feel better." Avaline leaned down and kissed her pale cheek. "And for reminding me what true happiness and trust look like."

"Come visit again soon, Avy; you are a good friend. I'll be praying for you." Layla sighed, and her breathing slowed to a peaceful sleep.

Avaline's vision blurred as she picked up her Bible and journal from the end of the bed and tiptoed out of the room, pausing to look back on the face of the most beautiful child she had ever met. A smile still rested on her lips.

Never had she seen such innocent trust. Never had she been so encouraged and challenged by the faith of such a young, beautiful soul facing such heartbreaking circumstances. Everything had crumpled on top of her and yet she never once doubted her Father's love. She trusted Him completely and rested peacefully in His arms.

"God, please help me to trust You like Layla. Even when everything falls apart, help me to love You like Layla does."

With one last smile at her young friend, she wiped away the tears streaming from her eyes and softly closed the door.

With her thoughts still and peace stealing over her soul, she started back towards her mother's hospital room. She paused with her hand on the doorknob. "Jesus, even if You take her home, I trust You." She rested her head on the door as tears of surrender rolled down her face. "You can take everything away if You want." Her voice choked. "I still trust You."

Taking a deep breath, she opened the door and slipped inside, going to kneel at the bedside. Mama still lay motionless on the bed, but Avaline detected a hint of color on her cheeks.

She took the chilled hand between her own. "Jesus, you know how much I love Mama. She's the person I love the most in the world. But I love You more. I trust You."

Avaline turned and sat with her back against the bed, holding out her hands palms up. "I trust You, Jesus. I trust You with everything."

Her phone dinged again, and she remembered the message that had so enraged her. *Do I dare read the rest of it? What hurtful words does he have to say this time?*

A voice seemed to whisper to her soul. *Trust Me.*

"I do. I trust You." Avaline closed her eyes and took a deep breath. She slid the phone out of her pocket and swiped up to unlock it.

Hey sis! Sorry it's been a while. I dropped my phone in the Mississippi. And I can picture your expression right now. You don't have to believe me, but I am telling the truth this time. Anyway, here's my new number. It's been a hassle to get one when I'm traveling around so much. The sights have been great. Wish I could take you on a hike up some of these mountains!

I know we parted on not-so-friendly terms, but I've had some awesome experiences in my travels and met some really cool people. I started reading my Bible again and I wanted to share this verse I read this morning. **Psalm 91:2: "I will say of the Lord, He is my refuge and my fortress: my God; in Him will I trust."** *Remember when we memorized this chapter together after Dad's death? It was a great comfort to me, and still is. I hope it will be to you again as well.*

Avaline's hand covered her mouth as fresh tears streamed down her face. But this time they were tears of joy. She could barely read the message that had just come through.

Oh, and my plane lands tomorrow at eight. I'm coming home!

Her phone slipped from her hand as she sat in shock. Reed was coming home!

All she could speak was a whisper. "Jesus, thank You!"

Feeling a sudden burden, she opened her Bible right there on the hospital floor. Then she sought out her backpack in the corner and dug through it to find her sketchbook. Turning to an empty page, she began drawing.

She drew a dark sky. Clouds blocked the sun. Rain fell in torrents. She drew a city—a crumbling city, with collapsing walls and falling rocks. And right there in the center of it stood Jesus, holding back the walls and the rain, His arms outstretched. Then she drew herself, arms around Jesus' waist, looking up at Him with an expression of total trust, yet with tears of grief streaming down her face. With a smile she added Daddy, bruised and beaten from the car accident. Then she drew Mama, pale and sickly from unknown afflictions. And finally she penciled in Reed, with clothes torn from the world's pleasures and lies. Finally, she sketched Layla, sitting at Jesus' feet, her young body riddled with cancer. Yet her face was radiant as she read aloud His Word from her worn pink Bible.

Avaline laid down her pencil and looked over her work with a small smile. Despite the world's trials and griefs and struggles, there they were, all gathered under Jesus's arms, completely safe and secure. Closing her book and sliding it into a protected place under the corner chair, she picked up her phone and typed out a reply to Reed.

Words cannot express what joy your message brings to me today. At first I was angry. Really angry. But I know you don't understand why. I'll tell you when you get here. I'm so glad you've started reading your Bible again. I need to read more often. Maybe we can read together? That verse has started to take on a whole new meaning for me. I love you, big brother!

Oh, and when you land, head to the Memorial Hospital. We're in room seventy-eight.

She slid her phone back in her pocket. Then, picking up the Bible, she laid it open beside her mother and, starting with Psalm 91, began reading aloud through the Psalms. A quiet peace settled on her heart. She brushed away a tear. Oh, what joy came from trusting Jesus when everything was falling apart!

THE END

EVERYTHING
BY BETHANY GRIGGS

SHIFTING FROM ONE side of the bed to the other, Caylee rubbed her aching shoulders and collapsed onto the pillows propped behind her. She picked up her phone and pulled down the notifications from the top. Two new texts. One from Jada and one from Anna. Tapping on Anna's text, she read the short message.

I didn't get to go shopping today after all. Woke up sick. Feels like the flu. My cousin went ahead without me.

Caylee frowned. She knew Anna had been looking forward to this outing for a while, and she was sorry for her friend's disappointment. At the same time, though, she felt a trifle hurt. Why did her friend have to bring this up with her? Sure, Anna had missed out on shopping today and would be disappointed for a while, but she would get well in a week or two and have plenty of future opportunities to go on other outings.

How long has it been since I've gone on an outing like that? After pondering the question, Caylee decided that the last time was probably the momentous day she had gone to a restaurant with her parents over a year ago. Unless you counted doctor's appointments, of course. Anna would soon recover, but *she* didn't have hope of ever being well again. So, why should she be the one encouraging Anna? Shouldn't it be the other way around?

Deciding not to answer the text right away, Caylee instead opened Jada's message.

Can I come over tonight? I have some news to share with you.

Caylee sent a thumbs-up emoji before tossing the phone onto the rumpled sheet. The sinking sensation in her heart matched her certainty of what this news would be. How was she supposed to act excited when her best friend was going to fulfill the lifelong dream they had shared and always hoped to do together?

Squeezing her eyes shut, Caylee dabbed at the tear that forced its way from under her eyelid. She wanted, oh, so desperately to be able to have something to offer others. But what could she give to anyone when she couldn't even take care of herself? How could she help people as she had always wanted to do when she couldn't even walk out of the house by herself?

Suppertime arrived and brought in Mom with a steaming bowl of potato soup.

"You need anything else?" Mom asked, positioning the pillows behind Caylee to prop her up.

"No. Jada is going to come over tonight. She has news."

Mom's face became an instant blend of sympathy and sadness. "Don't let it drag you down, Sweetheart. God still has a plan for you right here."

In bed? I just don't see it. Caylee kept her thoughts to herself.

It was just a few minutes after Mom left the room when Jada came in and sat on the edge of the bed, careful to not shake it more than necessary.

"How you doin' today, Caylee? Looks like you're well taken care of." She nodded her chin at the bowl of potato soup sitting on Caylee's bedside table.

"There's plenty more in the kitchen."

"Thanks. Your mom offered it to me on my way in, but I already ate."

Caylee blew on a spoonful of soup and waited for it to cool. "It's not been the greatest day, but I've had worse. What's your news?"

Jada pushed her thick, black braid over her shoulder and pressed her lips together. "You know, right?" she asked softly.

Caylee nodded. She felt sure she should say something, but she was afraid that if she did she would cry, and she had already made up her mind that this was not going to happen.

"They contacted me this morning and want me in Algeria helping out at a hospital by the middle of next month." Jada paused and rubbed Caylee's shoulder. "I know there is no way for me to fully understand everything you're feeling right now because I've never been in your place. But I do know you're hurting and disappointed, and that is something I have experienced. Still am in fact. It's not easy for me to leave you behind when we were going to go together. It's not easy for me to leave all that is familiar and go among strangers where I won't know anyone."

She stopped, her gaze fixed on the assortment of pill bottles cluttering the dresser top, her brown eyes swirling with emotion and unspoken words. Then she turned back to Caylee, speaking animatedly.

"I don't understand, but I do know this. God has a reason for me going, and He has a reason for you staying.

He's given us both something to do and share, and for right now, yours will be here at home, and mine will be in Africa."

Caylee nodded. She knew Jada was right, but somehow the words couldn't reach any farther than her mind right now. Her heart still felt empty and untouched. She managed to smile and ask questions about Jada's upcoming trip, but she was glad when her friend left for the night.

Two days later, Caylee had yet another doctor's appointment. This one was with her cardiologist. She always felt out of place in this office because the other patients were typically almost half a century or more older than she was. This time seemed to be no exception.

After her mom positioned her wheelchair in the waiting room, Caylee leaned an elbow on the armrest and propped her head up with one fist, absentmindedly watching the home renovation show playing on the television across from her. Instead of paying attention to her surroundings, she sat wishing her appointment was over.

A bubbly voice beside her shook her from her thoughts.

"It's a beautiful day today, isn't it? One of the nicest I've ever seen."

Who is so excited to be at the doctor's office? She must not be a patient. Probably just brought someone. Caylee lifted her head and looked at the girl in the chair next to her wheelchair. No, she probably wasn't a patient. She didn't even look as old as Caylee.

"How are you today?" Caylee smiled faintly at the girl, shifting in her wheelchair as a sudden pain reverberated through her legs.

"I'm doing just wonderful. I woke up this morning, and the sun is shining, and we have good doctors to help us, and life is just wonderful."

Maybe for you, Caylee thought. "I'm glad you're having a good day." The longer Caylee looked at the girl, the more she began to rethink her conclusions. The girl's face was pale and thin, and her eyes did not have the sparkle that should be there to match her voice—perhaps she was a patient after all. "Are you going to see the doctor?"

"Yes, I sure am. I didn't think I would be seeing him again, but here I am. And he's still here, too, and I'm happy about that."

Her enthusiasm was starting to wear on Caylee, and it was a relief when Mom took the seat on the other side of her wheelchair and conversed with the girl.

The girl seemed to have plenty to talk about, though she never got past little things like the breakfast she'd eaten that morning, the light traffic on the way to the hospital, and other trivialities.

"Caylee Ellis," the nurse called from the doorway. Caylee's mom stood up to push the wheelchair, but before she could start, the girl leaned forward.

"May I give you something?" She held out a small square of paper toward Caylee.

Caylee took it and slid it into her pocket. "Thank you."

After the appointment, Caylee was so physically and emotionally exhausted that she never even thought of the paper until after her nap at home. Slipping her hand into her pocket, she grasped the small, slightly crumpled square and brought it out. It was a sticker. The background was sunny yellow, and its white letters read, "Saying thank you to the King, whate'er each day may bring. Finding new ways to be giving, in anything and everything."

That's interesting. I guess that's why she was so happy and bubbly and gave me a sticker. She was finding ways to give in a doctor's office. That takes creativity all right.

Caylee turned over the sticker, revealing a few sentences on the paper backing.

I'm so thankful our paths crossed today and we got to talk. For me, each new day is a day to say thank you and give all I can to anyone I meet. I am terminally ill with cancer, and the doctors thought I would be gone before this. Each new day is a gift, and I want to give this gift to others. What about you? Will you share your gift with someone else today?

Caylee carefully turned the sticker back over and tried to reread the poem, but the words blurred and ran down with her tears. That girl who had talked to her and was so carefree was going to die?

I just felt sorry for myself and didn't say one encouraging word to her. Yes, I'm sick and always in pain, but I don't have any reason to think I'll die soon.

Caylee reached for her Bible on the shelf beside her bed and opened it. She would use this sticker as her bookmark. The Bible opened to where she had been reading in Second Corinthians chapter nine the day before. A few words caught her attention. "God loveth a cheerful giver . . . ye, always having all sufficiency in all things, may abound to every good work . . . being enriched in every thing to all bountifulness, which causeth through us thanksgiving to God."

Laying her Bible across her chest and clutching the sticker in one hand, Caylee turned her eyes to the ceiling. "Thank you, God," she whispered. "You've given me everything I need for giving to others. You put me here for a reason, and now I want to give my gifts to someone else. To many others."

After resting a little while longer, Caylee picked up her phone. She needed to return Anna's text. *I'm so sorry you're sick and missed the outing. Are you feeling any better? How can I be praying for you?*

Then, she sent a text to Jada. *I'm happy God has opened this door for you. I can't go with you, but I'll be there in spirit, praying for you often.*

A text from Jada came back immediately with a hugging emoji and two hearts accompanying the message. *You don't know how much that means to me.*

It wasn't long until Anna texted back. *Oh, Caylee. Being sick is the least of my worries. My family is falling apart, and I don't know what to do.*

Caylee sent up a prayer for her friend and texted back. *Can I be a listening ear for you? I'm here for you, friend.*

She smiled. *That's something I can give. My time. I may not have much energy or brain power, but what I have is a gift, and I can share it.*

Before Caylee had time to send any more texts, Mom came in with lunch.

"Thank you so much," Caylee said with a big smile.

Mom stooped down and gave Caylee a hug. "I haven't seen you smile like that in a long time, Sweetheart. It does my heart good."

After Mom left the room, Caylee stared at her sandwich. A simple smile could make that much of a difference? She could give that to everyone she met. True, she might not always feel like smiling, but if she was going by how her body felt, she didn't feel like it now either. Exhaustion and chills were already setting in from her trip to the doctor, and her pain levels were rising. And yet, she had smiled—and gotten a smile in return for the one she gave away.

A smile crept across her face again. What else did she have to give? This was becoming a fun game that made her more excited every minute.

Her eyes landed on the book next to her Bible on the shelf.

I told Allison thank you when she gave me the book, but I could also write her a thank you note. Maybe say a few encouraging words about how generous she always is.

Caylee snapped her fingers, so focused on her thoughts that she barely winced at the twinge of pain in her fingers. "Compliments!" *Of course, those are something free I can give away, and I know from experience that they make a difference.*

The next few days, Caylee kept a list of the things she could think of that she'd already been blessed with and could give to others. True, she was often at home alone, but even so, that didn't stop her from sending a text, saying a prayer for someone, or writing a little note for her mom to mail.

Less than a week after Caylee's impactful doctor's appointment, Jada came by for a visit. When she came in, Caylee was writing in an encouragement card, but she immediately laid it aside and smiled warmly at her friend.

"How is it going getting ready for your trip?"

"Fine." Jada clearly wasn't thinking about her trip. She looked at the note Caylee had set aside and then back at her friend's face. "You don't have to stop what you're doing just because I came in."

"But I want to. I'm happy to give you my full attention. I just love your sweater by the way."

Jada sat on the edge of the bed. "You look like you're feeling better today."

Caylee continued to smile, flexing the throbbing hand that had held her pen and rubbing an aching shoulder with the other. "My body isn't, but my heart is. Today is a gift, and I'm giving as much of it away as I can."

EVERYTHING
BY ANGIE THOMPSON

THE ROBINS WERE coming back for the winter.

She had known they would. Had never thought for a moment that they wouldn't. And yet somehow the sight of that first little red-breasted visitor hunting its dinner amid the remnants of her garden stopped the careful strokes of Miss Kate Hamilton's broom for fully a quarter of a minute as she watched it. Only when the bird turned one round eye on her and cocked its head curiously, as if asking the reason for her silence, did Miss Kate wake from her reverie and begin her sweeping again.

"Well, birdie, and what news d'ye have for me this year? The wee ones are grown long since; I know it in my head, though I can't seem to feel it in my heart. Have they bairns of their own yet? A trio of curly-headed lasses for Minnie, perhaps, and a sturdy lad or two for Duncan? Ach, I want to know it all. Do tell me everything."

She paused a moment, slowing her strokes as though listening for the reply, then began speaking again.

"Then Alec would be old enough for a family now, wouldn't he? Unless some cruel girl's broken his true, loving heart. Nae, I'll not think it of her, whoever she is. She'll be good to him; I don't see how she could help it. They'll have a wee lassie perhaps, with her father's bonnie eyes, and a babe with a dimple in his cheek. And young Edith—has her wedding day come at last? A big church affair, or a quiet one at home? Ah, she'll be the light of his life in any case. I only hope he's worthy of her."

Miss Kate came to the edge of the porch and leaned on her broom, watching the robin poke among the drying vines.

"I've little news of their cousins to send back with ye, I'm afraid. Though mayhap by the time spring comes I'll have heard from one or another. Rafe Evans says he met Lee in Corpus Christi a few months back, so at least he's not broken his stubborn neck on one of those wild mustangs—or hadn't." She shivered a little at the thought, then offered her visitor a sad smile. "Ye'll have all my own doings summed up in a week, I'll warrant. Does it pain ye, I wonder, to leave all your friends in the north for such a lonely place? Would ye do aught else, if ye could help it?"

The robin hopped to the corner of the house, ruffling its wings before cocking its head once more toward the porch, and Miss Kate shook her head with a sigh.

"Nae, birdie, I'm a silly old woman is all. Don't fret your bonnie head over me. But I've a loaf of fresh bread cooling in the kitchen. If ye'll come back tomorrow, I'll save ye the crumbs. Ye must have news to spread elsewhere, so I'll let ye be at it."

"Have you had news come, Miss Kate?"

The broom clattered to the porch as Miss Kate whirled to face the source of the voice, then placed her hand to her heart with a gasp.

"Joseph Carruthers, what d'ye mean giving me such a fright? I ought to bell your neck, playing such tricks with an old woman's heart!"

"Aww, Miss Kate, you're no older'n my ma, and she'd tan me good for ever calling her so." The young man took a step closer and leaned against the porch rail, sporting the sunny grin that always melted the icy edges off a scolding, no matter how well deserved. "I heard you talking and thought you might have company, but next time I'll remember to bust in like a herd of bulls, same's Ma's always telling me I shouldn't."

Miss Kate huffed as she picked up her broom and set it inside the door, slapping Joe's arm off the rail on her way.

"Did ye want something, lad, or are ye dawdling here to duck your chores at home?"

"Miss Kate!" Joe put a hand to his heart and tried to look aggrieved, but his twinkling eyes spoiled the effect. "All right, I've come for a purpose. I'm driving out to Everly to put in Ma's winter stock, and I thought you might want to come along, or send a list by me if you'd rather."

"Ach, is it that time already? And the robins back too. Aye, lad, I'll come if ye'll not mind my company. Will ye give me a moment to get ready?"

Joe nodded, and Miss Kate hurried to her room to change into her best town dress and check that her graying bun was still tidy. After fastening her straw hat securely with both ribbon and pin, she took down her little jar of savings and transferred a part of its contents to her small handbag, then set a folded paper filled with her careful script on top. This done, she rejoined Joe next to his family's wagon and accepted his hand to climb to the seat.

They rode in silence for long moments, Miss Kate busy with the remnants of her morning's musings and Joe apparently absorbed in some sobering thought of his own. But after a while, Miss Kate turned to her companion and offered him the inviting smile that had always endeared her to the young folks of the neighborhood.

"Something amiss, laddie? Ye look as though it's the world's cares ye've been given to solve today, and not a wee trip to town."

"Miss Kate." The words came slowly, and Joe turned to survey her with an unusually grave face. "When I startled you just now, were you—talking to the birds?"

"Ach, Joe, lad, it's not that terrible, is it?" Miss Kate attempted a light laugh, but it faltered a little. "If I couldn't talk except to a human guest, my voice might lose itself altogether. And the robins—well, they're a wee fancy of mine."

Joe cocked his head curiously, and Miss Kate turned and looked out across the endless plain as the scenes spread before her memory.

"It was just as I'd been asked to come here, and my niece Edith and the girls in the Sunday school were crying that they'd not be able to run in with all their little troubles, as lassies do. Well, I'd happened to read a piece the week before on how the robins spent their winters in Texas and other southern places, and so we hatched a plan that the robins would be our messengers—tell me all about them when they came in the winter, and tell them all about me when they returned in the spring. It was only play, of course, but the girls took to the notion, and so every winter when the robins come, I think of all the dear ones back home and make believe they've come with my messages."

"Miss Kate—" Joe's voice was hesitant, and he chewed at his lip for a moment before he continued. "You'll tell me if I'm being impertinent, won't you?"

"Aye, ye know me well enough for that, laddie." Miss Kate kept her tone soft, and Joe raised his head to meet her eyes again.

"Then why don't you go back? What's keeping you here now that Lee and the rest are gone? It's not the house you care about, is it?"

"Nae, Joe, it's not the house." Miss Kate blinked back a hint of moisture at the picture of the youngest of her sister's brood pausing on the threshold to remark, "Oh, I suppose you can have the house, Aunt Kate. It's not worth much with most of the land gone," before tying his bedroll to his paint gelding and trotting out of the yard with nary a glance behind him. "I'll not say I've not thought of it, but the truth is, I've nowhere to go. I've not heard a word from my brother's family in all of seven years. Like enough they've scattered as much as the McCoys have, and I'd not find them if I tried."

"When's the last you heard from *them*?" A muscle in Joe's jaw twitched ominously. "Any of the McCoys, I mean. And anyone saying they've seen one or another somewhere don't count if they didn't specially send a message."

"Stuart wrote last year." Miss Kate tried to speak with her accustomed cheerfulness, but somehow it seemed doubly hard after her talk with the robin today. "Ye knew he's struck a rich claim in Alaska?"

"He wrote to *you*? Or to ask Lee to come join him?"

"Lee was already gone, so it's little matter." She sighed and laid a gentle hand on Joe's tense arm. "Don't blame them too much, laddie. They never asked for their mother to be crippled, or for me to have to come. Stuart and Agnes were nearly grown from the start, and the rest used to seeing to themselves. They had little need of me." Even as she spoke, faded scenes rose before her eyes to put the lie to her words—long nights spent tending Ashby's broken leg, backbreaking hours poured into Julia's first "grown up" dress, anxious moments passed at the side of Lee's favorite broodmare when he'd sunk into an exhausted slumber in the straw. And yet somehow her heart had never been knit to the McCoy clan in the same way it had to Robert's family so long ago back in Connecticut.

"It just don't seem right." The troubled look didn't leave Joe's eyes as he turned them back to the horizon. "You coming all the way out here to take care of them, and then having no one left to take care of you. Seems you ought to be allowed to go home at least, after you've done what you came for."

For a moment, Miss Kate's heart clenched with the echo of his words, but she breathed a quick prayer and shook her head.

"Nae, Joe, lad. If the Lord saw fit to send me home, I've nae doubt He could manage. Mayhap in a few years, one of them'll need the old place to come back to, or mayhap there's some other purpose for me here. But it's not my part to know everything, only to walk faithful."

Joe swallowed hard and nodded slowly, and Miss Kate squeezed his arm.

"Now tell me, how is Evalyn Porter? I've not spoken to her in a month, but I'll warrant ye have."

"Oh, Miss Kate!" The young man's face flamed red, but his grin returned, and he allowed the subject to be turned away from her troubles and on to pleasanter topics.

The rest of the ride was filled with trivial, cheerful talk, Miss Kate having regained her equilibrium and knowing instinctively how to draw her companion out on the subjects that most interested him. In what felt like much less than the two hours the drive to Everly should have taken, Joe was helping her down in front of the large dry goods store and holding the door for her to enter.

Miss Kate's shopping was quickly accomplished and her frugal purchases safely stowed in the Carruthers' wagon. Joe finished loading the results of his mother's list, then glanced at the sky and down the street.

"Dad wanted me to stop in at the feed store to see about a new bridle and some barbed wire. Do you mind waiting, Miss Kate?"

"Nae, of course not, laddie. I'll walk down to the depot and have a look at the town. Take all the time ye need."

Joe climbed back into the wagon with a little salute, and Miss Kate set off at a moderate pace, marveling as always at the changes that had taken place since she had last visited a year since. New buildings were springing up on every side, and the stream of people and horses in the streets had swelled considerably, but thankfully the railroad was still in its place, and she had no trouble finding the depot. When she reached it, the train from San Antonio was just in, and the platform was filled with busy porters, hurrying travelers, and eager families.

Miss Kate stayed at the edge of the confused mass, keeping her eyes open as she always did when she happened upon the railroad, but of course Ashby was nowhere in sight. It was foolish to expect him. Likely he worked some other line entirely; five years without the slightest glimpse made it more than probable. But something still held her gaze on the puffing engine and drew it down the track after the caboose, where it lingered until the last of the smoke had disappeared.

"Lord, protect the lad wherever he is." She whispered the prayer beneath her breath and turned to start back the way she had come when a little cluster of passengers on the mostly deserted platform drew her notice. The wife held a whimpering baby in one arm and clutched a child of perhaps two against her skirt. Her husband's head was bent wearily, and his arm rested on her shoulder as though it was a necessary support. No family crowded around to welcome them, and no wagon stood waiting to bear them home.

Miss Kate's heart squeezed with compassion, and she took a step toward them, unwilling to leave even strangers alone in their trouble.

"Are ye waiting on someone, then? Or can I help ye in any way?"

The young woman's head snapped toward her, and her mouth fell open, but no words appeared. The young man lifted his gaze more slowly and blinked hard before whispering, "Aunt...Aunt Kate?"

The words were familiar enough, but her mind had been so set on Ashby, her eyes so intent on searching out a thatch of McCoy auburn that it took a moment for the stranger's light brown curls to focus. Then, with a gasp, her arms were around the thin figure, pressing him to her heart as though she might never let go.

"Alec! My Alec! Are ye true, laddie, or am I dreaming? What miracle's brought ye here, when I never thought to see ye more? Ach, whisht, lad." This as Alec's shoulders began to tremble in her grasp. "Whisht, my wee bonnie barra. Bide a bit and tell me all."

A fit of harsh, rattling coughs shook Alec's gaunt frame, and he turned away and fumbled for a handkerchief. His aunt loosened her grip enough to study him closely for the first time, and her brow knit in sudden concern.

"Why, laddie, how worn and white ye look! Whatever's happened? Come rest a moment. All of ye." The last was spoken with a sudden glimpse of the young wife— her Alec's wife!—hovering half anxiously and half shyly at his side. Scooping up the carpetbags that lay at their feet, Miss Kate kept her other arm anchored around Alec as she led the way to the quiet waiting room, moderating her usual pace to match Alec's lagging step and the child's toddling legs. When they were finally settled on a bench, she knelt in front of them, and her nephew sent a mute look of appeal at his wife, who nodded and reached over to squeeze his hand with the one that no longer clasped her little son with a death grip.

"I—I don't suppose you remember me at all, Aunt Kate?"

The voice was not any that had been born with a right to that name, but there was something familiar in it for all that. Miss Kate half closed her eyes and let her mind trail back over the years before opening them wide to take in the ebony hair, the pointed chin, the green eyes full of wistful longing but that still held some faint trace of their old mischievous twinkle.

"Why, Ivy Gray, as I live and breathe! Ach, are my eyes failing me, lass, or is it ye in the flesh? And the wee ones are yours—and Alec's?" She held out her arms to the little boy, and after only an instant's hesitation, he flung himself into them and nestled against her neck as though he'd always belonged there.

"Yes." Ivy's eyes glistened with unshed tears. "That's Bobby you're holding, and we—we call the baby Kitty. We thought—" Her words were cut off by another bout of coughing from Alec, and she shifted the little one into her other arm to gently rub his back. "Oh, Aunt Kate, I want to tell you everything, but is there a hotel nearby? It's been such a long trip, and Alec's so very weary."

"Where are ye bound, lassie? How soon before ye'll need to move on?" The words wrung Miss Kate's heart, but Ivy shook her head helplessly.

"There isn't—we've no special plans. It was all so sudden—the cold snap came on so fast—the doctor said

Alec couldn't bear another northern winter—and all we could think was to follow the robins south to where Aunt Kate had gone. As to finding you—we prayed so hard, but we scarcely hoped—"

"Whisht, lassie." Miss Kate reached out to caress the girl's bent cheek with her free hand. For a moment, sorrow threatened to swallow her, but it was quickly vanquished by a fierce resolve. "It's two hours home from here. Can Alec bear that, or d'ye need to rest in town a few days first?"

"Are you...are you sure, Aunt Kate?" Alec nearly choked the words. "What will our...our cousins say? We never meant—"

"Nae, ye never meant it, and neither did I, but the Lord did." His aunt's hand gently stroked the curly hair back from his ashen brow. "I'll not hear of ye moving on before we've made ye well and strong again, and there's none in the house but me, so I can do as I like with it. Ye'll not kick against it for the sake of pride, will ye, laddie, when He's worked everything so well?"

Alec managed a weak shake of his head before a coughing fit seized him. Miss Kate smoothed his hair until he was still again, then patted Ivy's knee in quiet reassurance.

"Ye ought to be in bed this minute, laddie. I don't know Everly so well since our mail moved to Fulton Corners, but I can find ye a boarding house. Let me—"

"No, please, Aunt Kate." The words were a whisper, but they somehow carried more strength than Alec had achieved before. "I'll be all right. Will you—take us home?"

"Aye, home it'll be, then." She swallowed a lump in her throat as she stood. "Ivy, let me take wee Bobby to bring the wagon while ye stay here with Alec. I'll not dawdle; I promise ye that."

"I don't know how to thank you, Aunt Kate." Ivy

wiped at her eyes with her free hand, and Miss Kate waved the thought away.

"We'll speak of it later, lass. There's plenty of time. Come, Bobby, lad, let's find that scamp of a Joe and see what room he still has in his wagon." Miss Kate lifted the child to her hip and set off in the direction she'd come, watching carefully for Joe or the feed store and smiling at the half-intelligible prattle of the youngster, which intensified every time a new wagon or rider passed them.

"Ye like horses, do ye, laddie? I've none left, I'm afraid, but when your father's a mite stronger, we'll see about it. Ben Singleton promised once to hold a colt for me, and it'll be just the thing to keep Alec out in this bracing air. Mayhap we'll find a wee filly too docile for cattle work so that Ivy can ride along. Think of it! My sweet Alec with naughty Ivy Gray! Ach, but the girl's changed wonderfully, that's evident. Like enough the Lord found a teacher to manage her better than I could. Nae, but I'll not be the one to plant stories in your head, laddie. Aye, that's a fine large one, isn't it? Ach, Joe, lad! Can ye squeeze me in the wagon bed for the trip home, d'ye think?"

Joe Carruthers's honest young face bespoke pure astonishment as he surveyed his erstwhile passenger from the wagon seat.

"I think I see myself letting you! Are you *trying* to earn me a hiding, Miss Kate?"

"Nae, laddie! If ye can't fit us all, I'll ask at the livery. Could their man drive us, d'ye think? Ye know I'm nae hand with a team."

"Miss Kate." Joe's tone hovered on the edge of worry. "What are you talking about? And when did you take to kidnapping?" He eyed the little boy on her hip with undisguised bewilderment, scanning the street behind her as though waiting for its parents to appear.

Miss Kate laughed. She positively could not help it.

"It's nae wonder ye think I've gone daft, lad. I'd think it too, if not for this bonnie wee bairnie of my own flesh and blood wriggling in my arms. Whisht, my wee barra." This to the child attempting to squirm away to reach the off horse of the Carruthers team. "D'ye want to ride behind the bonnie horsie, Bob? Aye, and ye may if ye keep still. Give us a hand up, Joe. I'll explain on the way to the depot."

Joe still appeared mystified, but he took the child, who had gone miraculously still at the promise of a ride, then leaned over to help Miss Kate up to the seat. She settled an arm around Bobby, and Joe clucked to the horses and turned them in the direction of the depot. When they were fairly started, Miss Kate turned back to Joe and attempted to put the day's revelations into rational order.

"I know I sound a mite off my head, laddie, and I'm sorry for that. My family's come, and I'm a bit giddy is all."

"Your family. You mean Lee? Julia?"

"Nae, not the McCoys. The Hamiltons. At least, Alec Hamilton, my brother's boy. Of all days for your mother to send ye to town! The Lord was in everything, there's nae doubt."

"Your family—from the north?" The wheels of Joe's mind seemed to be stuck in a muddy rut, but at least he was making progress. Miss Kate refrained from shaking him and squeezed Bobby instead.

"Aye, Joe. My nephew from Connecticut. The laddie on the seat beside ye is my grandnephew, and I've only peeked at his wee mite of a sister. Alec's ill, and the doctor's sent them south. Ye'll help me get them home where I can tend them, won't ye?"

Joe didn't answer as he pulled the wagon to a halt at

the depot and tied the team, but when Miss Kate led him into the waiting room and introduced him to Alec and Ivy, his eyes cleared with understanding, and he offered no further remonstrance as he set to work shifting the load in the wagon to accommodate the three small trunks. When he finished, there was just enough room for Bobby to perch next to his great-aunt on top of a flour sack with a bundle of quilting fabric at his back, and Miss Kate's heart swelled to near bursting as Joe handed her the now happily cooing Kitty and went to help Alec and Ivy up to the high seat.

The drive back home held little conversation, as Alec appeared to doze against his wife's shoulder, while Bobby derived endless amusement for himself and his sister by playing peek-a-boo behind his mother's shawl. When he finally tired of this, he was content to lay his head on "Auttie Kape's" lap and listen to the old Scotch lullabies that had once soothed his father until his eyes finally drooped and closed.

So lost in fond memories and happy dreams had Miss Kate become that it was a distinct shock when the rocking of the wagon ceased and she looked up to find herself at home. Joe was grinning up at her, and amusement twitched at the corners of Alec's tired mouth. Ivy reached for her baby, Joe took little Bobby, and Miss Kate gave them whispered directions to the upstairs room that had once belonged to the girls, then led Alec down to the sunny back bedroom first built for her sister and later claimed by Stuart.

She had kept that one bed made and aired year after lonely year, more than half expecting Lee or Ashby to be brought home trampled under a mustang's hoof or smashed to pieces in a train wreck. But now as Alec closed his eyes with a grateful smile and a sigh that seemed to release the weight of the world, she felt that every hour of patient watchfulness had been amply repaid.

Miss Kate stayed at her boy's bedside until he slept, then crept up the back stairs and peeked into the children's room. Both were still napping soundly—Bobby wrapped in a quilt atop Julia's old bed and Kitty in a snug little basket next to it. Hurrying back down by the front stairs, she spied a note from Joe on the hall table, reading only, "You were right, Miss Kate. God knew. I'll be by to help if you need me." Smiling softly, she placed it in her pocket and followed the clink of dishes to the kitchen, where she found Ivy clearing up the breakfast things she'd left when she went out to sweep the porch.

"Ach, ye've nae need to do that, lassie." Miss Kate kept her voice soft, and Ivy turned to her with overflowing eyes.

"I can't help it. I can't begin to thank you. I've been so afraid—but now I almost know he'll get well."

"He'll have the best chance we can give him, lass. They say the air here works wonders, and ye and the bairns are just the reason he needs to keep fighting. And to have ye come on the one day of the year that I step foot in Everly— ach, the Lord's in it, surely."

"We'll have to tell the family. They'll be thrilled to know where you are—and how to write. Did you think we'd all forgotten you, Aunt Kate? Well, we haven't. Mother Hamilton blames herself entirely for losing your last letters. It was when their father was sick for so long, and then—" She broke off with a painful swallow, and Miss Kate gripped the back of a chair.

"Go on."

"He—he died six years ago. Before Alec and I—oh, Aunt Kate, I'm so sorry!"

"Nae, lass." Miss Kate drew an aching breath and

shook her head. "He's the Lord's own, and we've naught to mourn for his sake. So the letters were lost?"

"Yes, and then the bank failed, and they had to move to Boston. They did send letters, but to Everly, and you—"

"Aye, it was near that time Fulton Corners got the post office. And Robert's last letter came there, so I never thought—" Miss Kate shook her head. "And then I suppose my letters never reached them. Poor Jennie. She oughtn't blame herself. Why, if I'd known where ye were, I'd have sold this house long since, and then where would Alec be? Nae, lassie, it's been in the Lord's hand from the start. We couldn't possibly see how everything works together, but He can. I'd not trade that for the world."

In answer, the younger woman put her arms around Miss Kate and hugged her hard, and her newly found aunt held her close for a long moment.

"Just look at ye, Ivy. My wee Sunday scholar grown into the woman I always hoped ye'd be."

Ivy groaned and pulled away.

"Oh, Aunt Kate, what a little terror I was! How I must have vexed you!"

"Ach, ye were young, lass. That doesn't excuse your faults, but it's a condition that cures with time." She smiled down at the girl, and Ivy gave a choked laugh.

"Do you want to know what cured me?" She glanced out the kitchen window, and her hand fluttered to her mouth. "Oh, they truly do come! Aunt Kate, do you see? Do you remember?"

Miss Kate's gaze darted over the familiar view until it lit on a little red-breasted bird swaying on the rail of the empty corral.

"D'ye mean the robins, lass? Aye, I watch for them every year. I've never forgotten."

"Of course you wouldn't." Ivy shook her head, but her mouth curved in a smile. "I had a robin's nest just outside my window for years, and somehow every ugly word, every unkind thought, the question came, 'And how would you like them to tell *that* to Miss Kate?' It was all play, and I knew it, but the idea haunted me. Then later as I grew, I saw how foolish it was—to worry so much about that when God sees everything without being told. But it helped me somehow, when I was just beginning to care. And please God, I'm better for it."

"So ye are, lass." Miss Kate blinked back the mist from her eyes and gave her a fond smile. "Now go freshen up from that awful train, and then ye can rest or help me with dinner, whichever ye like."

Ivy glanced down at her dusty traveling dress and obeyed with a rueful laugh, and Miss Kate cast a look out the window as she reached for the last of the dishes.

"And not a word did ye say that ye'd brought them along, ye wee scamp of a birdie. Ach, well, perhaps it's for the best. After all, neither ye nor I knows everything."

EVERYTHING

BY CASSIE CRELEY

RUBY WALKED OUT to the garden, surveyed the empty earth, and wondered if the lack of growth meant the seeds had been killed by the late frost.

The sun had burned off the glitter of ice, leaving the rich soil damp and frustratingly bare.

There was not even a hint of green.

She sighed. Ruby really didn't want to waste money replacing all the packets of seeds, especially with her two younger sisters in college. She knew the seeds didn't cost much, but her parents were already struggling to pay for her ongoing treatments. Maybe the garden would just have to wait until her treatments were finished, whenever that may be.

She had been feeling a sense of obligation to get this garden right. To do something productive, to create something she could share. Plus, her parents had okayed her grandfather plowing up half the backyard so that she could give gardening a try. Grandfather had put in so much work getting the soil to the right consistency. And then, when Ruby's parents had come home, they had walked into the backyard and looked a little shocked.

Her dad had smiled ruefully. "I see Grandfather plowed up the *big* half of the yard."

Ruby was kind of hoping they wouldn't notice that Grandfather's estimate of fifty percent had been a little...exuberant.

Her parents had assured her it was fine, but Ruby wanted to prove that sacrificing so much of the lawn was worth it.

She was tempted to dig up a patch of the garden to find the seeds and check if they were rotten or not. This garden was supposed to be a *good* thing, not add more uncertainty to her life. But Ruby was new to gardening and wasn't sure if it was worth the risk of damaging the seeds. After all, the seeds might be just fine.

Patience, a Voice seemed to whisper to her.

Ruby closed her eyes, put her hands into her pockets to resist the urge to dig, and tried to imagine what was going on beneath the ground.

Maybe under the soil, each and every seed was blazing its own trail, myriad little roots reaching down and eagerly drinking up the melted frost. Maybe each seed was sending out shoots in the opposite direction too, each one reaching for the sun.

But what would grow? Ruby's imagination had a habit of running wild. In her mind, she suddenly pictured the backyard transformed by the seeds producing not little garden plants, but something impossible. She imagined tropical trees dripping with vines and vibrant pink flowers shooting up all around her. She could almost smell the fragrant fruit that would grow in such trees. As her imaginary forest soared higher and higher all around her, Ruby could picture colorful birds and playful lemurs flashing through the canopy. Ruby smiled at the unexpected and magical turn her daydream had taken.

Daydreaming seemed to be her hobby lately. At least she had the energy for that, and in her daydreams, at least, things turned out right.

Reluctantly, she opened her eyes and couldn't help but be disappointed by how her real-life hobby looked. No forest, not even a garden, just blank dirt.

Then she heard a scrabbling sound on the other side of the wood fence. She smiled, knowing what that meant.

Her little neighbor Tobin called out, "Is that you, Ruby?"

She had been babysitting him since he was two, and she still got the chance to from time to time now that he was seven. His voice was a welcome distraction from her disappointment.

"Hey Tobin," she said. "Come say hello!"

Tobin peeked over the top of the fence and waved. Ruby and her family all considered Tobin like a little brother, so he frequently ended up climbing the stump in his yard to chat over the fence. More often than not, he was asked to walk over and visit.

"Can I come see the garden?"

"Well, there's not much to see…but come on over."

In a flurry of noise, Tobin took off to race around the fence.

"Oh look, a leaf!" he exclaimed as he raced into the backyard. He poked at the far edge of the patch of bare earth.

"Wait, really?" Ruby asked, walking over. When she changed her perspective and looked at the garden from this angle, she could see there was indeed a little leaf, half covered by a clod of dirt.

"Oh, I see it!" Ruby exclaimed joyfully. "You found the first one!"

"Cool!" Tobin said. "What's it going to be?"

It was going to be a *garden*.

Hope filled Ruby as she was suddenly sure that the seeds were going to be all right.

Maybe she hadn't been daydreaming big enough...

Ruby leaned down and pointed at the tiny sprout.

She whispered to Tobin, "This row is going to be full of giant purple mushrooms, big as cars."

Tobin's eyes grew huge. "*Really?*" Then he caught the twinkle in her eyes, and he fought back a grin. "What about this row?" he asked, playing along.

"Dragon eggs," Ruby replied.

Tobin giggled. "How about this row?"

"What do you think?"

"Hmmm, palm trees! They'll grow pumpkins!"

They laughed, and Ruby could picture their wild garden. She stood up and walked Tobin along the garden, sharing with him what was really going to grow in each spot.

When they were at the opposite end, he asked, "What about blueberry bushes? Those are my favorite."

"I didn't plant any bushes. Those take a long time to grow."

"Like a hundred years?"

"No, not that long!" she laughed. "But I only got seeds, and a bush would take a few years to produce fruit."

"Is that a long time?"

"Well, not really, I guess, but I just wanted to try annuals at first." She couldn't really explain it. She wanted to build the garden from the ground up. And buying bushes felt like cheating. Plus, they would have cost more. And she hadn't wanted to commit to any plant that would take years to produce something, not when she wasn't sure if the garden would fail.

Tobin leaned down to check for any other leaves and found a pebble with swirls on its gray surface. He put it in his pocket.

"Are blueberries your favorite too?"

Ruby shook her head. "Raspberries are mine."

"You should plant some!"

"Well, maybe. I'll see how this year's garden does first."

Her garden quickly became her oasis. So much of Ruby's time was spent in bed or in doctors' offices, and it was more than a relief to have a place that felt like a world removed from all that. She didn't make it outside every day, but when she did, she could feel some of the weight leave her shoulders.

It seemed painfully slow, at first, waiting for more to grow. Hardly anything seemed to change.

Until suddenly, it did.

Soon there were distinct little rows of soft green all over the once-bare earth.

She would sit on her favorite bench along the back fence and wait with the seedlings for the sun to get warmer.

This afternoon, she was amazed to see more leaves sprouting on each row. The various rows of beans and peas now had curling tendrils reaching out in all directions, creating an ode to the color green.

Ruby took a deep breath, the heady scent of the warm soil and new plants creating a refreshing fragrance. She unwound the hose and walked into the middle of the garden.

Funny how most people felt that working with the earth made them feel grounded. She felt she had traveled somewhere new entirely. Something about the garden made her feel as though she were an astronaut, journeying alone to a distant planet. Out here, in the quiet, she felt outside the orbit of the normal cares that weighed her down. Maybe that was it—gravity felt a little gentler.

She turned the hose on to a light shower. It was a nice break, being able to care for something versus being cared for.

As she moved between the rows, she pictured herself on a deserted moonscape, bringing lifegiving water to the plants that would sustain her on the edge of space. She would be getting the outpost ready for new arrivals who would help her make this a thriving colony.

She looked up, trying to imagine what it would be like to see a glass dome above her if she were really living in an enclosed habitat far from earth. A breeze rustled through the trees and sent the little plants shivering. Ruby imagined it would be even quieter in space with no wind moving leaves.

In her imagination, Ruby envisioned a space colony made up of glass habitats dotting a desolate planet. She could picture herself leaving the confines of her dwelling-habitat to escape to her interstellar garden in the darkest part of the night. Then she could camp out next to the plants and smell the familiar fragrance of home while staring up at brand new stars.

Ruby smiled. Space sounded lovely. But she was also enjoying the view right here.

Summer inched closer. Ruby measured time in inches now, it seemed. The slow inches of a leaf unfurling, or the thread of a stem uncurling to become more substantial, until it was sprouting leaves of its own.

Ruby crossed the yard to sit on her bench. She stretched out slowly, trying to let her muscles unwind. She had planned on doing some work in the garden today, but she felt she barely had energy to even sit up. Yesterday's treatment had been especially draining.

She knew days like this would come, but that didn't make them easier. She just had to move through them, inch by inch.

But enough of that, Ruby thought. The garden was where she took a break from thinking about it, at least for a little while.

Ruby had never realized how many different shapes there were to the leaves of garden plants.

She really hoped all these plants did more than sprout leaves. To celebrate the end of summer, and to thank everyone for helping, Ruby was planning to host a salad-themed potluck.

Since she'd had the idea to start the garden, her family had asked if they could help. They'd created a calendar so they could take turns watering. Her grandfather and Tobin's parents had also volunteered to have their names added to several days.

On days when it rained, Ruby appreciated that God did the watering. Ruby always went to the calendar after a rainfall, crossed out the name listed, and replaced it with "God."

It seemed to rain most frequently on days when Ruby was scheduled to water. Ruby smiled at how often God helped her take care of the garden.

The sun was just starting to settle into Ruby's bones when she heard the sound of her sisters' voices as they climbed out of a car.

Her sisters rounded the corner of the house, and Carly sang out, "Look what we got!"

She was carrying two large plants, and Gabriella was carrying another.

Plants, when she had specifically set out to grow her entire garden from nothing but seeds.

Ruby felt oddly possessive, and she tried to squash the feeling. She had long ago accepted that she would need help with the garden, but still, she wanted it to be something that was *hers*. Her decision about what to plant, her project to manage, something she could control and get right.

But Ruby reminded herself that the garden project was actually more fun when it was bringing everyone together. She loved seeing her sisters so enthusiastic.

"Surprise!" yelled Gabriella as they plopped the potted plants on the ground.

Ruby smiled as her sisters reached her. "What did you find?"

"Tomatoes!"

"On sale," Carly stage-whispered.

Gabriella sat cross-legged on the grass by Ruby's bench. She gestured at the plants, "I know you didn't want to 'cheat' with a garden, but we really wanted to surprise you with something. Plus, we figured since this one plant is especially scraggly, it's less *cheating* and more of a challenge."

Ruby eyed the scraggly plant. Carly reached toward it and gave it a little appraising shake. Ruby was surprised no leaves fell off. The poor thing was half the size of the others, its leaves wilted, its branches few.

Ruby had to laugh. "That one does look a little like

190

Charlie Brown is about to put ornaments on it."

"Also," Carly pointed out, "You said you wanted to make a salad bar for the party you're planning. You *can't* have salad without tomatoes. And getting tomatoes from the store would *really* be cheating."

"All right, you've both convinced me," Ruby said, holding her hands up in mock surrender. Her sisters grinned. "Thank you both; this was really thoughtful of you."

"I knew you wouldn't be able to resist a plant in need!" Carly exclaimed. "So where are we going to put them?"

Gabriella must have noticed how tired Ruby looked, because she said, "Let's sit here for a little bit while we plan it out."

Carly looked back and forth between her sisters and nodded.

Ruby appreciated their patience, and they chatted for a while about where to put the tomatoes and how much they were looking forward to eating them later this summer.

When Ruby was feeling more rested, Gabriella went to fetch the bucket where they kept a small shovel and various gardening tools. Ruby and Carly picked a spot at the end of the garden where there was still some room. They began extricating the tomato plants' tangled roots from the small pots.

Her sisters started talking about their classes and grumbling about how much homework they'd have this upcoming weekend.

Ruby knew they loved school, but it was still a little hard to hear their complaining. She missed college. She missed the sense of possibility.

As they started digging holes for the plants, Ruby realized why their conversation struck a sore spot. They both had their own things. They both had school, of course. And Gabriella had her internship and hiking with her boyfriend. Carly had her volunteer project and her theater group.

She wanted something that was hers, as if being "the one who could garden" defined her. Maybe it was silly, but she wanted something to set her apart other than "the one who is sick."

Both her sisters were actually doing something with what they were learning in college.

Ruby patted the earth around the base of one tomato plant.

More than once, she'd been tempted to bury her own diploma out here in the garden. She'd imagined it would bring forth so many career opportunities, maybe the chance to travel. But the future seemed as blank as her garden when it was delayed by frost.

Patience, the Voice said again.

Ruby took a deep breath, calmness spreading through her. Maybe her future was just lying dormant as well.

Who knew what might still grow?

As she dusted off her hands, Ruby looked up to see her sisters had finished with their plants as well and were now goofing off.

She didn't want craving her own identity to rob her of enjoying this chance to spend more time with her sisters. She grinned as Gabriella tried to show Carly a bug on her hand and Carly leaped back with a shriek. The bug flew away, and they both shrieked again at the same moment, then burst out laughing. Ruby joined in.

That's who I am, the one with two goofy little sisters.

They gathered up the tools in the bucket and stood back to admire their work. The garden looked more complete now. Gardens grow, and they should grow people closer together, too, Ruby decided.

The tomato plants stood, like three sisters, two on either side of the wilted one.

"Now the garden is complete," Ruby said with a smile.

"There's still some room over there for—" Carly began.

"No more!" Ruby and Gabriella exclaimed. They all laughed and Ruby pulled her sisters into a hug.

"What's there to eat?"

Tobin had joined her again today, and she was enjoying his company as they pulled little weeds together. He had become a great helper.

"Nothing yet. The lettuce is almost ready, though…" She laughed as Tobin made a face. "You might like this lettuce. It's supposed to be kind of sweet."

Ruby stood and brushed off her knees. "Time to water! Can you dump the weeds into the compost for me?"

When Tobin returned with the empty bucket, he followed Ruby as she began unwinding the hose.

"I'll inspect the garden for you," Tobin said, walking ahead as Ruby started down the first row.

Ruby was instantly curious what his inspection would entail. "Sounds great!"

Tobin started walking around the garden, nodding to himself every now and then. He measured a few bean bushes and looked pleased that they were taller than his waist. He looked like he was a giant moving through a miniature ecosystem.

At her feet, the lettuce, spinach, and arugula looked like a minute forest beneath green foothills of carrot and radish tops. Next to Tobin, the taller beans and peas created a landscape of vibrant mountains dotted with the snow of white blossoms. Tobin gave them an affectionate pat. He was proud of helping her parents get the climbing plants propped up on fences.

Tobin moved to the end of the garden, which was bright with yellow flowers. Beneath the broad cucumber leaves, large starbursts of flowers were appearing everywhere. More yellow flowers covered the now-thriving tomatoes.

Tobin had reached the edge of the forest and now was among the part of the garden scattered with stars. Ruby smiled at the thought of him as an astronaut exploring the galaxy.

Tobin turned back to announce, "Everything's growing!"

Beside him, the tomatoes were so heavy with unripe fruit that she had to smile at their exuberance.

"It's all the help it's getting."

Tobin came back to join her.

"Yeah, and the *sun*." Tobin pointed out.

Ruby hid a laugh at Tobin's more pragmatic approach to gardening. She switched the hose nozzle to "off" as she made her way the next row.

Tobin stopped suddenly in front of her, and she halted just before she bumped into him.

"I think something's wrong with the carrots…"

Ruby peered at the fluffy green fronds, expecting mold or some other catastrophe. She leaned closer to the plants, which looked absolutely fine. Then she saw Tobin's puzzled expression.

"Oh, that's just the tops!" Ruby explained. "The

carrots themselves are underground."

"Huh." His tone implied he didn't quite approve of this method of growing.

Ruby could rather relate. She wondered how big the carrots were getting, if they were good. A lot of gardening was uncertain, and she was becoming more okay with that.

"It will be a surprise," Ruby mused, "when we pull them up."

"Hmmm," Tobin reflected. "Kind of like a piñata."

When the day of the potluck arrived, Ruby couldn't wait to show her family and Tobin's family all the produce from the garden. (Well, her sisters had already seen it—they'd helped her pick everything.) She had turned all the greens into giant salads that filled her family's two punch bowls. Various other vegetables, including a horde of tomatoes, filled other bowls so that everyone could pick their own toppings. The carrots, cucumbers, peas, and radishes looked as bright and inviting as confetti.

Ruby's mom had made a pasta salad and Tobin's mom had made a potato one. Ruby's dad grilled chicken to top the salads. Tobin had helped his dad choose all the best fruits for their fruit salad.

Grandfather had brought numerous salad dressings, along with croutons and bacon because he insisted that no salad was complete without them. Everyone agreed with this sentiment.

In keeping with the salad theme, her sisters had shredded carrots and made a lopsided but delicious-looking carrot cake.

Ruby was rather dazzled as she surveyed the colorful feast.

The meal was a great success. Everyone gathered around picnic tables in the backyard, savoring the summer sun as well as the delicious food.

As the last bites of cake were eaten, Ruby looked around at her loved ones, a smile on her face.

After the meal, everyone started tidying up. As Ruby was gathering up some dishes, her mom walked over to her side. "Why don't you rest awhile while we finish up?"

Gratefully, Ruby retreated from the hustle and bustle for a break. She was tired, full, and happy, and a quiet moment was just what she needed.

Ruby settled into her favorite bench and watched from across the yard as everyone finished divvying up leftovers. Her sisters were talking about what lawn game they should all play.

Ruby's eyes settled on her garden.

So many more vegetables were ripening.

She thought about how her imagination had run wild as she pictured what would grow here.

It was just an ordinary garden, full of ordinary fruits and vegetables. Nothing like something from outer space or a fairy tale.

And there was something magical in that. How something ordinary could grow, and nurture, and connect.

Everything around her was thriving.

Tobin had managed to slip away from folding tablecloths, and Ruby smiled as he climbed up on to the bench beside her. He looked out at the garden too.

"What are you going to plant next year?" Tobin asked her.

The future was full of possibilities.

"Everything!" she replied. "I want to add zucchinis, and watermelon, and…"

"And blueberry bushes!"

Ruby laughed. "Yes, and blueberry bushes. And raspberry bushes too."

EVERYTHING
BY A.Y. DANIELS

Prologue ~ Challenge Accepted

I'M ESTHER, WIFE of Jeremy McFarley. This story is for my daughters, MaryAnn Faith and Raye Ella.

I know it may seem funny to you that I'm writing a story. I've never been much for writing, but when Aunt Lilly challenged me to record my days in a creative way, I thought an educational story for you two would be the best thing to do.

I don't consider myself a great writer, so bear with me. I'm trying this thing out.

This particular story is about the crazy couple of weeks that led up to MaryAnn's twelfth birthday party. I tried my best to write it as it happened, and to honestly share with you my heart and my thoughts.

Chapter 1 ~ Phantom Shag

"Don't forget the stamps and ink, MaryAnn," I call from the kitchen.

I finish dinner prep and make my way to the living room. MaryAnn is busy looking through my box of scrapbook paper. She glances over as I fold myself cross-legged onto the floor.

I finger through some sticker pages that had found their way to the carpet. "Are we going to make textured or illustrated cards?"

"Ooh! Let's do textured cards. I'll go get some glue." Mary Ann hops up and bounces to the laundry room/craft closet. Just as she opens the door, a fluffball of white emerges to fly through the house.

I jump up and gasp. "Sprinkles!"

I proceed to chase down and grab the little menace. The phantom shag dashes behind the couch. Since she hasn't emerged on the other side, I assume she found refuge in the powder room.

I approach both hastily and stealthily before dropping down on my knees in the powder room doorway.

I expect Sprinkles to charge, but... Nothing?

"Oh, Mom!" MaryAnn is back at the table, wrestling her white Labrador. "She got in the glue!"

I pop up and twirl. Sure enough, the puppy is chewing on one of the glue bottles that MaryAnn had tossed over when Sprinkles escaped. I dash over and pick the brat up.

"Bad girl," I scold as I wrench the bottle out of Sprinkles' mouth. "Would you clean up the mess while I pen

Sprinkles up outside?"

"Yes ma'am." MaryAnn sighs. "Some of the paper is dirty now."

"Choose some others, Honey. It'll be fine." With that, I carry Sprinkles out.

MaryAnn and I are able to finish making the birthday invitations without any more interruptions.

When my husband, Jerry, gets home, I transfer the role of "child-supervisor" to him. I make sure dinner is close to being done and then begin to set the table.

As the girls wash their hands and sit at the table, I remember the pitiful puppy outside in the rain.

"Oh, dear. Just a minute and I'll be back," I tell Jerry and the girls.

I dash out through the French doors and trudge through the slurpy wet yard. "Sorry, Sprinkles. I'm not mad at you, really."

I only half notice that her pen is bent open some... Hmm.

I pick up the muddy lab (holding her at a distance) and carry her into the house. Jerry opens the laundry room door, and I set Sprinkles down. I pour a half scoop of feed into her feed bowl and then rub the dog with a towel.

"Sorry, girl."

Sprinkles licks my hand in forgiveness.

Back to dinner. I wash up and join my family at the table. We hold hands and pray, giving thanks for safe travel, a productive day, and the upcoming party. I then serve Raye, my six-year-old daughter, while Jerry and MaryAnn serve themselves.

"Ooh, Daddy! Do you think you could get us ice cream and cookies for the party?" MaryAnn fidgets in her seat giddily.

Jerry grins. "Sure, Annie-Doll." Pausing to take a bite, he turns to me and tilts his head. "What happened with Sprinkles today that got her put outside?"

"Oh… that." I can't decide whether to sigh, laugh, or blush at the whole situation. "Well… MaryAnn and I were going to make invitations for the party. When she went to get some supplies in the laundry room, Sprinkles escaped and got a hold of the glue. I put her outside… and accidentally forgot her as the afternoon wore on."

"Oh… I see." Jerry chuckles. "Well, the greatest of us fall short sometimes."

"Oh, stop it." I toss a broccoli floret at Jerry, play-frowning. "You know I'm not great. Otherwise, I wouldn't leave the poor thing out all day."

"I never said that you're great." Jerry bites his lower lip, clearly trying not to laugh.

"Oh, how *dare* you!"

"*You* said that you aren't great! Don't be inconsistent." Jerry attempts an innocent grin.

I sit back and smile. "All right, all right. You're *so* funny. I needed that laugh, though."

We settle down and finish dinner quietly. I have the girls clear the dishes. After loading the dishwasher and hand washing, we gather together for family devotions.

Jerry reads Philippians 2. It really stands out to me, especially the part about being grateful in all things.

I wasn't grateful when Sprinkles raced around, or when she got into the glue. But it gave MaryAnn and me an opportunity to exercise a bit and practice patience.

Thank You, Lord, for giving us that puppy. She's sweet and doesn't really know any better yet. Thank You for using her to build my patience. Help me to be more grateful... grateful in everything.

Chapter 2 ~ Sick

Early the next morning I start some coffee and take Sprinkles out for her walk. We walk out the front door and around to the back. My mouth drops as I stare at the flower beds along the house.

Well, I don't need coffee this morning to wake up.

Sprinkles guiltily avoids the area, likely feeling my astonished annoyance.

"Sprinkles? You did this? How come I didn't see it last night?" I sigh and almost whimper. "No. Be grateful... What's the good in this? I guess I can replant everything and implement what I've been learning about gardening. Come on, girl."

Finishing our route around the house, I put Sprinkles away, feed and water her, then grab my coffee and my Bible.

Jerry comes out of our bedroom, so I set my Bible journal aside and start his lunch.

When I hand him his lunch bag, I realize that neither one of the kids is up. It's already seven-thirty. Usually they're up and getting ready for school by now.

Hmm. I hope they aren't sick.

"Bye, Honey," I call as Jerry opens the door. "Um... The girls might be sick today. I'll call you if they are."

"Okey dokey," he says before waving goodbye and heading out to his truck.

I watch Jerry drive off before checking on the girls.

Peeking into their room, I see that they're still asleep. Slipping in, I notice that neither one is under their blankets as they should be. I kiss their foreheads to check if they have a fever. They're both hot to the touch.

I head to the kitchen and concoct some honey water and dig up some elderberry syrup. While I play mad scientist, I call Jerry.

I slip back into the girls' room and sit down on MaryAnn's bed. "Hey. You feeling okay, Annie-Doll?"

MaryAnn's eyes flutter open. She smiles and nods slightly. "Mm-hmm."

I feel her forehead again. "You sure, honey? You have a fever. And you've slept late."

"I'm okay, Mom. Just tired and cold." MaryAnn pushes herself up weakly.

"Stay in bed, Dear. Here's some medicine." I offer one of the cups of warm honey water and a spoonful of the elderberry syrup.

MaryAnn takes them well. I had no worries for her, but Raye might fight back.

I move over to Raye's bed and rub her back. "RayeBug. Dear, I need you to drink these goodies to help you feel better."

She rolls over and moans.

"Here, Raye." I swish the honey water around and check to see if it's still warm. "This tastes really good, but it's going to get cold."

Raye opens her eyes and grabs at my hand. I help her sit up and make sure she doesn't spill the honey water. Her face puckers, but she complies better than I expected.

"Thank you, Raye. Here's some syrup, before you finish the drink."

She moans again. "I don't like syrup."

"I know, honey. The water will make the taste go away." I tug at Raye's mouth until she opens it, and I manage to slide the spoon in without issue. "Thank you, RayeBug. Here's the water."

She winces and reaches for the cup. She gulps down the water without spilling any, to my relief. I rub her face as she settles back down.

I leave the girls in their room and go to drink some vitamin water, so I won't get too sick.

Thank You for…this time, Lord. While they're sick, I'll have some extra time to clean the house like I've been meaning to. You know best, Lord. Please get my baby girls better in Your timing. In Jesus' name, amen.

I return to my Bible journaling, somewhat grateful for the extra time alone. I prep dinner, sweep the kitchen, and check on the girls again. They're sleeping soundly.

I set up the sewing machine and work on mending until the girls wake up. I don't want to start gardening if they don't know where I am.

MaryAnn stumbles into the dining room and settles down beside me, wrapped in her fuzzy blanket. I set aside a skirt and give her a kiss. "How are you doing, doll?"

"Tired. My throat hurts." She leans her head against my arm and breathes heavily.

"Did the honey water not help, Dear?"

"It helped. But I don't know how long it's been since I had it. I think I slept with my mouth open."

"I'll get you some more. It has been over two hours." I get up and make some more honey water, then hand it to MaryAnn before I check on Raye. She's still sleeping, though quite fidgety.

I come back to the kitchen and mix a vitamin drink

for each of the girls. I set the bottles aside and turn to MaryAnn.

"When you're done, Annie, there's a vitamin drink for each of you. Would you mind watching Raye while I'm out replanting the flower garden?"

"The flower garden? Yes, ma'am. What happened?"

"Sprinkles must've gotten into it when I penned her outside yesterday. I guess her staying out worked as punishment in advance for ruining the garden."

MaryAnn nods, her expression quite blank. I gather what I need for garden recovery so she can get some quiet time.

Hopefully, the plants won't die from the shock. I guess I'll tidy things up if they're a hopeless case.

I walk out the door with my basket of tools and kneel down to work. As I pick up clods of dirt and straighten the fallen plants, I consider the recent incidents.

Why do things like this happen? Sprinkles nearly ruined my time with Annie yesterday. And she ruined the garden. Now I have to take time out of my plans and fix it. Now the girls are sick. We'll have to miss church and wait on party prep. I need to make sure some food is ready for when I go down, too.

I sit back and breathe. My muscles are tight and my nerves winding. *Father, Your plans are best. Mine cannot measure up. Help me trust You today and work in Your strength. In the holy name of my Savior, Jesus, amen.*

I continue thinking, remembering encouraging tidbits from God's Word.

Not everything will go according to my plans. But everything is in God's hands. And He can and will use everything for His glory. In His Word, He tells me that He works all things—everything— together for the good of those that love Him and that are called according to His purpose. I'm called by Him to be here for my husband and kids—through everything.

I relax, smile, and continue my garden repairs.

Chapter 3 ~ Icing on Sprinkles?

Now that it's a day before the party, MaryAnn and I are in the kitchen.

"Time for the icing. Want to get the butter and cream?" I grab a sack of powdered sugar from a shelf.

"Yes, ma'am." MaryAnn digs through the refrigerator and pulls out the ingredients.

I set up the stand-mixer and read over the recipe again. "Hmm... Okay, so first we need to 'cream the butter.' Ready?"

"Mm-hmm!" MaryAnn practically glows and bounces with eagerness. I chuckle before we get started.

I'm happy to say the process is clean (I'm notorious for messy icing-making) and smooth. Pun intended. I set the icing aside to rest. MaryAnn and I remove our aprons and hang them up.

"Okay. Let's take a break and clean your room." I grab some cleaning spray and a cloth. MaryAnn skips ahead and I follow close behind.

I set my tools down, surveying the room. "Oh, nice! It's cleaner than I thought. We should only need to dust then. We should be able to do it while Raye finishes her nap."

"Yay!" MaryAnn starts dusting her shelves and dresser, while I take apart the window and clean it thoroughly.

We tidy the rest of the room and throw some papers and other things away. We start talking as we near the end of our mission. Rather than carrying the conversation out of the room, I sit down on MaryAnn's bed and talk with her some more about growing up.

As the conversation winds down, I nearly forget the icing that needs to go to the fridge. But *someone* slips up and makes a quiet "*thump…thump*" noise in the kitchen. I stop mid-sentence and listen hard. Then…

CLANG!!!

"Oh, no." I hop up and run to the kitchen.

I freeze, and my heart drops to the floor with the weight of an anvil.

Sprinkles sits by the refrigerator. Her head is low. Guilt and icing are plastered all over her face.

"*Sprinkles!*"

MaryAnn comes up behind me and gasps. "Oh, Mom… I'm so sorry."

I'm going to cry.

All that work. All that time with my daughter. Ruined. Why do things have to come crashing down? Why can't the days stay normal with Sprinkles around?

I grab the dog and take her outside. She knows that she's guilty, so she isn't fighting or playing around, which makes hosing her off easier. Somehow, though, I end up randomly wet.

I bring Sprinkles back inside and ruffle her in a towel, then lock her up in the laundry room.

"I'm really sorry, Mom. I should have put her away before we went to clean my room. I guess I ruined the icing."

I frown and mutter, "Yeah, I guess." I shake my head and bow in prayer.

I shouldn't be upset. Please forgive me. She owned up to it, and we still have time to make the more icing. You have everything in control, even when it feels out of hand. Take it out of my hands and into Yours.

"I'm sorry for being snappy. Thank you for owning up to it."

MaryAnn smiles somberly, wasting no time in cleaning up the sweet mess.

"While you do that, I'm going to take a shower before we make the icing again."

I fly through the shower, trying to be careful to not separate myself from MaryAnn for long after the incident. She doesn't need to think that I'm upset with her.

We start making another batch of icing after I'm out of the shower. My bad mood lifts when I realize something.

I'm getting to make double the memories. I got to make icing once and have a good time, and now I get to have a good time again. Thank You, Father.

Jerry comes in from work as MaryAnn and I finish applying the crumb coat to the cooled cake. He sets his things down in our room as usual and returns to the kitchen. Raye stands close by, watching me and MaryAnn clean and admiring her play-apron.

Ruffling Raye's Dutch braids and patting my back, Jerry asks, "You okay, honey?"

I turn and set the cake by the refrigerator. Glancing at my husband, I tilt my head in confusion. "Yes, I'm fine. Why?"

"You were frowning when I came in. I hope you aren't upset with me about something."

"No, no! I'm not upset with you. I guess I haven't gotten over what Sprinkles did. I'm sorry."

"Oh? What did Sprinkles do?" Jerry takes us girls'

aprons and hangs them up for us.

"Well, I guess she knows what cake is supposed to look like. I think she was trying to add some Sprinkles to the icing, and instead got icing all over herself."

Jerry presses his lips together and chuckles. "She sure does know how to turn things around. Next it's going to be Sprinkles versus cake."

"Please. The thing seems like she's able to absorb thoughts and ideas through the walls *and* understand them."

Jerry laughs and wraps me in a hug. "It can't be that bad."

"Just wait." I shut my eyes. I'm really not joking.

Chapter 4 ~ Sprinkles and Gratitude

MaryAnn and her friend, Julia, dash from the girls' room to the backyard. Before I can call them, I hear an excited knock at the door.

More guests. How many families did we invite? Was it nine? Oh, dear.

I shuffle to the door, dust my apron, and welcome the family of five in.

When they flow through the house into the backyard, I start bringing out the chips, buns, condiments, sauces, little candies, goodie bags, and drinks.

At last, I get to take out the cake. MaryAnn and the kids are playing with Sprinkles now. She'll be too busy to notice the cake… I hope.

I set the dessert down and go check on the barbecue.

Jerry is leaning over the grill, checking the hot dogs and burgers. I pat his arm, and we exchange smiles.

One of the parents walks up and greets me. We talk about our kids and their grades. We end up discussing our past week, and right as I'm ending the "Icing on Sprinkles" story, I hear squeals and a yelp.

Turning, I see the famous menace of a furball leaping onto the table. Some of the little girls are squealing in delight, but the older kids are frozen. Sprinkles smashes the cake and starts to eat it. A dad at the table jumps up and snatches the puppy away from the crumble-mash.

I run over to the crime scene with the woman I was talking to.

Grabbing Sprinkles, I mutter, "Oh, you—you rat."

Sprinkles hangs her head and whimpers. I thank the man and then excuse myself. I go into the house and set Sprinkles in the kitchen sink.

She's unusually compliant, so I just take a minute to breathe. I rest my head on the counter. My core shivers as a tear slips down my cheek. My thoughts run wild.

Now is not... not the time. But why does everything go wrong just when it starts going well? I don't get it. I'm tired of it. I just want a day—a week—that's normal.

Sprinkles squeaks as she breathes. She turns a circle in the sink and rests her head beside mine. I look up and splutter a laugh.

"Why do you have to be so cute?" I roll my eyes and stick my tongue out at her. She sits up and "smiles."

Being the party-pooper that I am, I utter Sprinkles' least favorite words. "Time for a bath."

She doesn't take too kindly to that, but she doesn't try to escape. I guess with all the trouble she's gotten into, she's used to taking baths.

When she's all clean, I rub her down and lock her in the laundry room. As I approach the back door, I catch a glimpse of furry icing on my blouse. Walking into the hall to look at my reflection in the full-length mirror, my jaw drops. There's fur and icing and crumbs all over me, not to mention the fact that my sleeves are soaked.

I trudge sulkily into my room and grab some clothes. After changing, I check my hair, wash my hands, and rinse off my face.

Back at the party, I see some parents talking with some of the younger kids, but MaryAnn and Raye are still chatting and playing with the others. When my girls notice my return, they excuse themselves and come to talk.

"I'm sorry about the cake, Mom." MaryAnn hangs her head, looking disappointed and guilty.

"It isn't your fault, Annie." I embrace my now-twelve-year-old daughter, frowning in thought.

"What about the cookies and ice cream that Daddy got, Annie?" Raye offers, leaning against her sister. "Couldn't we have those for the party?"

I smile and agree. "I remember that. Didn't you want those, MaryAnn?"

MaryAnn ponders for a moment before offering a smile and nod.

This Friday morning is quiet. It's warm enough that I sit outside with some hot tea (I am *not* a coffee addict like some may say). Despite the occasional road-noise, I savor the peaceful morning noises. Noises that keep me from going crazy with the storm in my heart.

No matter how much I pray over these thoughts—these *angry* thoughts—there is no way to silence them. I stand and grab my things before heading inside.

Maybe it will be easier to read in my normal spot, I hope.

I open my Bible to Philippians. I start out reading chapter two, but I suppose God is prodding me on to read to the end. After pondering some, I do a search on a Bible app.

The word "everything" is on my mind. Honestly, it has been for days. So that's what I search for.

A few verses stand out to me:

Casting down imaginations, and every high thing that exalteth itself against the knowledge of God, and bringing into captivity every thought to the obedience of Christ… (2 Corinthians 10:5)

Be careful for nothing; but in every thing by prayer and supplication with thanksgiving let your requests be made known unto God. (Philippians 4:6)

In every thing give thanks: for this is the will of God in Christ Jesus concerning you. (1 Thessalonians 5:18)

And a passage from my normal reading that caught my attention is Philippians 2:12-16:

Wherefore, my beloved, as ye have always obeyed, not as in my presence only, but now much more in my absence, work out your own salvation with fear and trembling. For it is God which worketh in you both to will and to do of his good pleasure. Do all things without murmurings and disputings: That ye may be blameless and harmless, the sons of God, without rebuke, in the midst of a crooked and perverse nation, among whom ye shine as lights in the world; Holding forth the Word of life; that I may rejoice in the day of Christ, that I have not run in vain, neither laboured in vain.

I'm hit by the fact that I haven't been appreciative as I should have been, especially in the chaos.

I've been entertaining grouchy, ungrateful thoughts. I haven't been going about my days obeying Christ as I dream of when I sit to read His Word and pray.

I'm not being a shining light in this dark world or my falling nation. I likely would not be a joy to the mentors who have taught me over the years. Am I a joy to my husband and children?

I haven't been leaving everything in God's hands—I have been worrying over situations, circumstances, and the little brat of a dog we have. Rather than giving thanks for the hard situations and asking for the Lord to live through me, I've been selfishly complaining.

I—I've been rebelling against the will of God!

I gently push my Bible and journal out of the way and drop my head into my hands.

"What is wrong with me?" I clench my jaw and press my eyes closed.

"Sin nature, honey." Out of nowhere, my husband slips into a chair beside me and rubs my back. "We aren't supposed to be perfect. We can't be." Jerry hugs me and pulls me close. "We're supposed to let go of our works, our plans—our will—and surrender ourselves to God, so that He will work in us, live through us, and so we become like Jesus."

I bite my lip as more tears gather and escape. "It's so hard."

Jerry sighs and hugs me tighter. "I know... What was it that we read in James last night?" He slides my Bible over and turns the pages to the book of James. Clearing his throat, he begins reading softly.

"'Do ye think that the Scripture saith in vain, The spirit that dwelleth in us lusteth to envy? But He giveth more grace. Wherefore he saith, God resisteth the proud, but giveth grace unto the humble. Submit yourselves therefore to God. Resist the devil, and he will flee from you. Draw nigh to God, and He will draw nigh to you. Cleanse your hands, ye sinners; and purify your hearts, ye double minded. Be afflicted, and mourn, and weep: let your laughter be turned to mourning, and your joy to heaviness. Humble yourselves in the sight of the Lord, and He shall lift you up.'

"All it takes is trust. Nothing we can do—even trusting or praying—can earn favor in God's eyes, or get Him to answer our prayers, or get us to be more like Him. 'For by grace are ye saved through faith; and that not of yourselves: *it is* the gift of God: Not of works, lest any man should boast.' It isn't works that save us, and it isn't works that keep us saved or loved by God."

I force my eyes open and consider those last words. *Loved by God.*

My heart warms and flutters. "You're right... Thank you, Honey."

"Of course, Love." Jerry pats my back, and with a heavy sigh, he stands and grins. "So, what's for lunch?"

I smile—beam—and even snort. My hand flies to my mouth. Jerry's grin spreads. He gives me another hug before I get up to make his lunch.

Lord, thank You for teaching me about Your love, Your strength, Your patience, and Your will. I want to be thankful. I'm going to stop trying to be grateful and happy in my own strength. You take control and work in my heart. Thank You... for everything. In Jesus' name, amen.

Epilogue ~ Challenge Completed

It isn't a long tale, but it was a *long* couple of weeks. Honestly, I don't know how I endured Sprinkles' misadventures other than by God's grace.

And trust me, it wasn't just those two weeks that she

was a wild child. The little puppy that we got a mere six months before this story did turn out to be an...interesting guard dog two years later. For that I am grateful.

But just because those two weeks were hard, rough, and challenging, does that mean that God wasn't good? Does it mean that He didn't care, or that He wasn't there?

What do you think? What does God say?

When my father and my mother forsake me, then the LORD will take me up. (Psalm 27:10)

Let your conversation be without covetousness; and be content with such things as ye have: for he hath said, I will never leave thee, nor forsake thee. (Hebrews 13:5)

Many there be which say of my soul, There is no help for him in God. Selah. But thou, O LORD, art a shield for me; my glory, and the lifter up of mine head. (Psalm 3:2-3)

Whether you're one of my daughters, relatives, or someone entirely different, know that God loves you. He will always be with you.

Be grateful, trusting, and believing... always and in everything.

There you go, Aunt Lilly, MaryAnn, and Raye. Challenge completed, for the glory of God and the teaching of my daughters.

The End

EVERYTHING

BY SHERRICE MYERS

Operation Everything

"WHAT ARE YOU doing?"

"Exactly what it looks like."

"That's what I was afraid of…"

Talia looked down at her friend Elora who was fluttering about gathering a bunch of random objects. Elora's arms were filled with a myriad of items. Talia was just about to comment on them when she saw her friend's wings swing dangerously close to her mother's favorite vase. "El, watch your"—CRASH—"wings…"

Talia glided down to where Elora had toppled over a glass vase, its once-sparkling fixture now shattered into hundreds of shards strewn across the floor.

Elora gasped. She dropped the items in her hands and flew over to where Talia was holding a shard. "I'm so sorry Tal… I was just so distracted and lost track of where my wings were."

Talia sighed. "It's okay, Elora. Besides, it looks like you have other things to worry about." She glanced over at the pile that Elora had abandoned.

"What's all that for?"

Elora waited a moment before answering, focusing intently on cleaning up the mess she had made. She blew some pixie dust on the shards, then waved her hand, commanding the shards to come back together into the vase. One by one, the shards pieced themselves together until the vase was whole and then drifted gently to its shelf, settling into place.

Once that was complete, she dusted her hands against her skirt petals. "Well, it's Quinn's birthday tomorrow, and—"

"Wait, what?" Talia stepped back in surprise. "How did I not know about this?"

"I didn't know either until I overheard Chef Hattie ask if he'd like a pixie blue cake or a dragon green one for his birthday tomorrow."

"Wait, Chef Hattie knows too?" Talia sat on the ground. "How did we not know about our own friend's birthday?"

"Well, Quinn doesn't talk that much, especially about himself."

"Well, we have to fix this. Birthdays are special. And Quinn is special too. Everything has to be perfect." Talia stood up and clapped her hands.

Elora smiled and held out her hand. "Operation Everything is ready to commence!"

Talia took her hand and flew out the door, pulling Elora behind her.

"Favorite color?"

"Dragon shell green."

"Favorite place?"

"Everglade Park."

Talia fluttered back and forth asking questions, writing the answers down on her notebook. She bit the tip of her pencil. "What else are we missing?"

"I don't know of anything else yet. We have the decorations and the cake is being made by Chef Hattie... Wait... That's it!" Elora sat up on the mushroom stump she was lying across.

Talia dropped her pencil in surprise. "What? What is it?"

"Guests!" Elora snapped her fingers. "We have the place and the decorations, but we don't have any people!"

Talia smacked her forehead. "That's right! It wouldn't be a party without the people!"

Elora began to fly about, counting on her fingers. "There's Chef Hattie, Herbmaster Charlie, Watchman Will..."

"What about our flying class partners?" Talia asked.

"Oh! That would be great." Elora smiled and took a piece of paper from Talia's notebook. She leaned over it and wrote frantically. "There's Elyn, Zeke, Amelie..."

"Are you saying all our classmates' names for a reason?" a boy's voice spoke from behind the two pixies.

Talia and Elora gasped and turned around, hiding the papers behind their back. In front of them hovered Quinn. His silver hair glinted in the sunlight and his thumbs were tucked around the straps of a pair of mouse-hair overalls. Usually, the sight of their friend would make them happy; however, this time, the girls were at a loss for words.

"Well...we were...uh..." Talia looked at Elora for help.

"We were trying to list some of our favorite people throughout our village." Elora took her piece of paper from behind her back. "See?"

Quinn took the paper and looked it over. "Cool!"

"Yeah, it's for a project we are working on!" Talia jumped in.

"Fun, can I help?"

"NO!" both girls cried out in unison.

Quinn looked between the two of them, startled. "Oh. Okay." He handed back the paper to Elora. "I guess I'll let you get back to it then." He turned to fly back towards the village when Elora called out. "Wait, you can help with this part."

"Really?" He turned back around, eyes hopeful. "Yeah, who are your favorite people in town?" Elora smiled, holding the paper out to him.

He took it and the pencil from Talia. He tapped his chin thoughtfully then wrote down two names. "I should let you guys get back to the project. I'll see you later?"

"Absolutely!" Talia nodded.

Quinn folded the paper and handed it back to Elora. "Good luck on the project!" He flew away.

"Who'd he write?" Talia flew over to look at the paper as Elora unfolded it. The girls smiled as they looked at the two names written in Quinn's handwriting.

Talia

Elora

Elora looked at Talia. "Well, I guess that means we are invited." The girls laughed and then continued writing names.

The next order of business was to get the invitations out to those who would be coming to the party. The hardest part? Quinn was everywhere the girls needed to be. Talia sighed in frustration. "How are we supposed to invite people to the secret birthday party without the birthday boy finding out about the secret birthday party?"

Elora slipped an invitation onto the sill of an open window of their classmate Lillybeth's house. They ran into the shadows just as Quinn flew by, helping Farmhand Gary herd the fluttercalves through the streets. Talia and Elora giggled as the "moos" of the purple and green fluttercalves called out to the passersby. One of the calves caught sight of the two girls and fluttered in their direction.

"No no no!" Elora let out a hushed whisper.

The girls shooed the fluttercalf away from them. The winged creature looked at the girls curiously and tilted its head.

"Hang on! One of the fluttercalves went in this alley." Quinn's voice called out.

"Oh no!" Talia said. "Quick, hide!"

Talia pulled Elora behind a stack of barrels. The girls listened as Quinn came over to the calf. "Hey there fluttergirl. Whatcha doin over here?"

The girls gently peeked out from behind the barrel to see Quinn kneeling by the calf, stroking her between the wings. The fluttercalf licked his hand. "You're cute, but we need to get you back to your friends."

"Moooooo." The fluttercalf turned and walked back to the rest of the herd with Quinn following close behind.

"Aww…" Elora whispered. "He was so gentle with her."

Talia laughed. "Guess we need to add a fluttercalf to

the guest list."

Elora joined Talia's laughing and shook her head. "Even if we wanted to, we are out of invitations."

The village bell chimed and the girls listened to the amount of rings. "Five?" The girls looked at each other.

"We are going to be late for supper!" Talia cried out. "And the party is in two hours!"

"Don't worry, Operation Everything will be a success. You'll see!" Elora said. She grabbed her friend's hand and began to fly towards home. "We can eat supper and make it to the meadow early!"

"Elora, you're a genius!"

After supper, Elora and Talia rushed around trying to finish all the last-minute details of the party.

"I have the caaaaaaaakkkke" Chef Hattie sang out, revealing a green dragon egg cake surrounded by little cakes with little dragons frosted on them.

"These are amazing!" Elora cheered with delight.

Talia clapped her hands excitedly, "Bring them over here; they will be at this table."

Talia turned and saw Lillybeth, Zeke, and a few other classmates standing there. "Hey guys! I'm glad you could make it"

"Thanks for inviting us! We had no idea it was Quinn's birthday. Where do we put the gifts?" Zeke asked.

The girls hearts' sank as they looked in their friends' hands and saw small gifts wrapped neatly and covered in bows and pixie dust.

"Right, the gifts..." Elora swallowed hard.

"Um…you can put them beside the cake." Their classmates nodded and headed towards where Chef Hattie had just placed the dragon cake and was now shooing away Farmhand Gary's fluttercalf.

Talia turned to Elora. "Oh Elora, how could we forget gifts for a birthday party?!"

Elora sighed and sat down on the mushroom closest to her.

"Now, everything is ruined…" Talia sat down beside her. "Everything…"

Suddenly Village Master Clarence called out over the crowd, "Now presenting the birthday boy, Quinn!"

The girls looked up to see a stunned Quinn looking over the large gathering of friends here to celebrate him. Everyone cheered and clapped as Quinn was led to where Chef Hattie had lit the candles on the birthday cake. Elora smiled gently as she saw the birthday boy's eyes grow wide with wonder.

"Well…maybe not everything."

The next hour or so was filled with music, laughter, cake, and games. The smiles on everyone's faces told the girls that the fairies were having a great time. Elora and Talia were especially happy to see that Quinn was enjoying the party. But when it came time for the gifts, Talia and Elora hung back on the edge of the crowd, not wanting to be seen.

Quinn noticed and flew over to them. "Hey, what's the matter?" He looked at the girls.

Elora's eyes brimmed with tears and her wings drooped. "We…forgot to get you a present."

"We were so busy trying to get the invitations out without you seeing us, it slipped our mind." Talia looked down. She fidgeted with her flower petal skirt. "We were trying to make this the best birthday we could and..."

Talia was cut short as Quinn pulled Talia and Elora into a tight hug. "Guys, you did a great job. You didn't need to get me a gift. You putting this together was the best gift I could ever hope for."

He let go and Elora wiped her eyes. "Really?"

Quinn smiled. "Really. Everything is perfect."

"Everything?" The girls looked at each other.

"Everything."

EVERYTHING

BY LUCY PETERSON
AND ALAINA JOHNSON

MAGGIE WALTERS SAT in the stiff pew, her eyes on her worn black shoes. She didn't dare to look up at the sombre ebony coffin before them. She would only burst into tears again. And she didn't need that. Not now.

She needed to be strong.

For the twins' tear-streaked faces beside her.

For Mum, sitting next to them, alone.

For her brother Arthur, who had suddenly become the new man-of-the-family.

But how could she be strong when Daddy was no longer there to lean upon? When his body lay cold inside the wooden coffin, his life stolen by a single bullet, never to laugh, to hold her in his strong arms, or to twirl her across the kitchen floor again?

Why did it leave such an empty spot inside her?

Why is everything falling apart?

Maggie looked up numbly, barely registering that everyone around her had risen.

The yellowed pages of song books rustled and

throats cleared.

Maggie slowly rose to her feet as the organ began the chords to Daddy's favourite hymn.

> *Oh Lord, my God, when I, in awesome wonder*
> *Consider all the worlds Thy hands have made,*
> *I see the stars, I hear the rolling thunder,*
> *Thy power throughout the universe displayed.*

She couldn't avoid looking at the closed coffin in the front of the room.

Tears stung her eyes again, and she tried to sing bravely, but her voice faltered as she heard Mum's waver beside her.

> *Then sings my soul, my Savior God to Thee,*
> *"How great Thou art, how great Thou art."*
> *Then sings my soul, my Savior God to Thee,*
> *"How great Thou art, how great Thou art."*

The words broke from her throat in catching sobs. She couldn't stop the tears from flowing as she choked out the melody. *I miss you, Daddy.*

When the tears blocked her voice completely, a strong arm wrapped around her shoulders, pulling her close. She glanced up at her brother's tearstained face. Nothing in the horrible past few days shook Maggie more than watching Arthur break—her big brother who had always been stronger than her.

She buried her head in his arm, her quiet sobs drowned in his sleeve.

It seemed as if the song went on for hours, an unending reminder of Daddy. Eventually it faded, but still

Maggie did not look up.

Arthur squeezed her close, and she felt his cheek rest a moment on her head. "Come on, Megs," he whispered. "We have to go."

She sighed. Pulling out of his arms, she straightened and wiped her eyes with the back of her hand. Nodding, she turned to follow what was left of her family out into the aisle. She didn't look up to meet anyone's sympathetic gazes as they walked solemnly up the aisle. Tears sprang to her eyes again as Arthur's rough hand gripped hers.

Bright sunshine brushed her face as they stepped outside.

A young man stood by the open doors, fingers fidgeting with the brim of his hat. He stepped forward. "Mrs. Walters?"

Mum smiled sadly, holding out her hand. "Lieutenant Lewis. What a surprise."

"Yes, ma'am," he said, taking Mum's hand in a gentle shake. "I got an unexpected leave. I'm sorry I didn't make it in time to attend the funeral." He glanced at the church, sorrow filling his eyes. "Oscar was a good man, ma'am. A very good man. The best friend I ever had." He shifted sideways. "I just wish that bullet had hit me instead."

"Don't wish that." Mum laid her hand on his arm. "Oscar held you back for a reason." Tears glimmered in her eyes. "He gave up his life for his men in that skirmish. Don't waste that gift with regret."

He looked up and nodded, but Maggie could still see the guilt weighing him down.

She backed away from the small group that formed around her dad's best friend. She couldn't bear to hear him reminding her of how her father had died. Her thoughts scrambled away from her.

What—or who—was there to lean on when everything fell apart?

She watched as Arthur turned away from the group. He beckoned her to them, but she turned away and stared at the ground.

A second later Arthur appeared beside her, gently wrapping his arm around her shoulders and resting his chin on her head. She buried her head in his side again, trying to hold back more tears. When she looked up, she found that Liuetenant Lewis wasn't standing before Mum anymore. She searched the crowd and found him standing before her father's coffin, his hat clutched in his hands and his head bowed.

Hearing a sniffle beside her, she turned to see Thomas. He reached for her hand. "I miss him," he whispered.

"I do too." She knelt down and hugged him.

A gentle hand rested on Maggie's shoulder. Maggie looked up to see Mum standing over them. She smiled sadly. "It's time that we be heading to the gravesite."

"Yes ma'am." Maggie stood, grabbing Thomas's hand. "Come on."

Black.

Maggie shuddered. She now detested that colour with every fibre of her small body. There was nothing left in her life but black since the funeral last week.

Black clothes. Black thoughts. Black feelings when she caught Mum crying over one of Daddy's old shirts.

She sighed before leaving her room and closing the

door behind her. Clattering down the steep steps of their flat, she pushed through the tiny hall into the side parlour.

"Mum, is Arthur home yet?" She plopped down on the small crimson settee, sending a look of disgust at the black curtains hanging over their window. She hated the job her brother had been forced to pick up when Daddy had joined the army. "Mum?" She glanced up. Then she froze.

Mum stood beside the low grate, tears streaming down her deathly-pale face as she stared at a small note held in her shaking hand.

"What's wrong?" Maggie jumped to her feet.

"A courier just brought this." Mum looked up, her voice wavering. "It's Arthur."

"What?" Maggie rushed to Mum's side. "What happened?"

"There's…" Mum looked up, taking a slow breath. "There's been an accident."

Maggie could feel her face pale. "Is he okay?"

"I'm… I'm afraid not."

"Mum! What do you mean?" Maggie grabbed her arm. "What happened to him?"

"I don't know." Mum burst into tears. "He's at the hospital."

"The…" Maggie breathed, stepping back. How could her brother—her big brother who had never been laid down by anything in his life—be in the hospital?

"I… I have to go to him." Mum said, looking around. "He'll need me."

"I'll watch the twins," Maggie responded. She wrapped her arms around Mum and gave a quick squeeze. "Go."

Maggie tried to keep her breathing steady as she paced the tiny front hall and messed with one of the buttons on her white blouse.

Thank goodness the twins are with Mrs. Hilblum.

She felt as if her stomach was in her throat. She could barely breathe, feeling like she was stumbling through a fog.

Mum had come home late that night only for enough time to find a coat and see the twins off to bed.

She had also brought the awful news.

How could he have lost a leg? Maggie couldn't comprehend it.

That was a month ago... and still she was too shocked to cry.

She jumped as footsteps sounded on the walk outside. *Is it them?* Rushing to the door, she peered through the small peephole.

It was just a passing neighbour.

She sighed, running her hand down her shoulder-length brown bob. Stepping into the side parlour, she restlessly plumped up the pillows lining the settee for what felt like the hundredth time. Mum said Arthur would have to sleep in the parlour until he had recovered enough that they could turn something on their ground floor into a new bedroom.

After all...how could someone with only one leg climb stairs?

That thought sent a fresh wave of numbness through her. Arthur... never able to climb stairs again? How could he continue in... anything?

A sharp rap at the door interrupted her thoughts.

"Oh!"

She rushed into the front hall, racing with shaking fingers to unlock the old oak door. Pulling it open, she stepped aside, squinting at the rush of cold air that blew in.

Mum stepped through the door first.

"Megs," she whispered, wrapping her arms around her.

Maggie squeezed back, nearly bursting into tears at the sound of Arthur's pet name for her. "They're here," Mum said, pulling away and peeking out the door. "Are you ready?"

Maggie bit her lip. Her mother's words sent a wave of panic through her, but she nodded. Arthur would want her to be strong.

The door swung open, and a man backed into the house, lifting the edge of a cot. Maggie gulped. She would be strong. She *had* to be.

But at the first sight of him, her breath caught in her throat. She fled, clattering up the steep, dark stairs to her tiny room. Slamming the door behind her, she fell face first onto her bed. She couldn't face it yet. She wasn't ready.

A part of her told her that as soon as she saw him it would all become terrifyingly real. Sitting up on her neat quilt, she pulled her legs up under her tweed skirt. Stinging tears dripped down her nose.

A soft rap tapped her door, and it creaked open. "Maggie?" Mum peeked her head through the doorway. "Are you all right?"

She took a deep, shuddering breath. "Yes."

"He's awake." Mum stepped all the way into the room, shutting the old door behind her. "He wants you, Maggie."

"I…" Maggie shook her head. "Tell him I'm coming."

"How about you tell him yourself?"

Maggie sighed, sliding off her bed. Her stockinged feet hit the cold floor with a muted *thud*. "Yes, ma'am."

Her feet felt heavy as she dragged them down the dark stairs. She was unable to look up. Slowly, she crossed the front hall and stopped before the closed parlour door.

She couldn't run away this time.

Laying her hand on the cold knob, she slid the door open.

"Megs?" A low voice greeted her ears.

She stepped into the parlour, shutting the door behind her. Somehow she couldn't bring herself to look at the settee.

"Megs?" the voice said again. Arthur's voice... but different.

She turned slowly. To her relief, a sheet was draped over his legs—or... leg.

"Hey, Arthur." She moved over to his side, kneeling next to the settee. Her breath caught in her throat.

He looked... so different. His usually unruly brown curls lay limp against his grey-white forehead. Deep lines creased across his weary face, making him look so much older than his fifteen years.

"Hey," he rasped, grinning. "I missed you."

"How..." She stopped. What could she say? She hadn't seen him in a month. And he had lost a *leg*. "How are you...feeling?"

"What do you think?" He pushed up to face her, voice growing bitter.

Maggie drew back. "I..."

"No... no. I'm sorry." He closed his eyes, shifting against the pillows. "It's not your fault. It was a crazy mistake I made."

Maggie's heart ached at the bitter regret in his voice.

"What... what happened?" she hesitated.

Was that the right thing to ask? She shifted uncomfortably. Why did her big brother suddenly feel like a stranger?

"I..." He shook his head. "It doesn't matter."

"Ar—"

"No, Megs." He opened his eyes, pain radiating from their cold surfaces. "Do you even realise what happened? I lost a leg. A *leg*." He looked down at the thin white sheet covering his leg, face constricting. "I'll never be able to do anything again. *Anything*."

Maggie gasped for breath, kneeling frozen and small before this stranger that was supposed to be her brother.

"Yes, you can," she gasped.

"I can't!" Arthur yelled, straightening. "Megs, I can't. They said I won't even be able to walk. I'm no help anymore!" He winced, falling back. "I'm just a burden to you all."

Maggie scooted back, stunned tears running down her cheeks.

Never before. Never before had her big brother yelled at her.

"Arthur..." she whispered.

"Stop." He closed his eyes, turning away. "Just... stop."

Maggie reached up to wipe her burning eyes, numb fingers trembling. "Do..."

"No. Just go away."

Maggie pushed to her feet, rushing out of the room. She raced up the stairway, her heavy footsteps drowned out by choking sobs. Mum's call for her was silenced by her slamming door. She fell onto her bed with a cry of heartache.

Arthur's words kept running through her head.

I'll never be able to do anything again.

Maggie pulled her tweed coat tighter around her to shield her from the winter breeze. She ran down the walk, her Mary-Jane shoes clattering against the stone. Her short hair blew wildly in front of her face as she clutched the sheet of paper closer to her body.

All across London these posters hung.

She ran up the stone steps to their flat, sliding a key out of her pocket and shoving it into the brass keyhole. The lock clicked loudly before she pushed the door open and—not waiting to take off her coat—dashed into the parlour.

Mum sat in the old armchair by the window, nestling a cuppa in her hands. Arthur was propped up with pillows and staring at his lap. Their attention turned to Maggie as she breathlessly ran in.

"Mum!" She held out the poster before pulling off her coat. "What is…" She stopped when she glanced over at Arthur and realised what was in his lap.

"You've already seen it?" She didn't look at her brother but met Mum's teary gaze. "What's it all about?"

She stepped closer to Mum and gazed at the crumpled paper, her eyes drawn to the huge stamped headings.

Save the Children!
Evacuate England's young!

"What does it mean?" she asked again.

Mum sighed. "I was hoping to keep this from you children. I hoped it was just rumours."

"What rumours?" Arthur said, sitting up and turning

his head towards them. "Mum?"

Mum didn't speak for several moments, staring at her tea. "Cities in England are being bombed. The people talk of… war."

"War?" Maggie stepped back. "In England?!"

"Like the Great War?" Arthur asked.

Mum closed her eyes. "Yes."

"Again?" Maggie glanced between her and Arthur. "But that was only twenty years ago."

"Yes. England hasn't healed enough for another war so soon." Arthur murmured.

"Does…" Maggie glanced at the poster. "Does that mean we have to leave?"

"You and the twins do." Mum said.

"But… but what about Arthur?"

He laughed shortly. "You forgot, Megs? I can't walk."

Maggie gritted her teeth and dropped her gaze, his words reopening the slow-healing wound in her heart.

"Arthur can't be moved like that yet." Mum reached out, her finger tipping Maggie's chin up. "Maggie, I wish this didn't have to happen. But…" She stopped, brushing away tears. "Be strong for the twins."

Maggie nodded, her eyes burning. She forced them back. "When do we have to leave?"

Mum sighed. "I don't know. You had better pack a case."

"ALL ABOARD!"

Smoke billowed from the engine, sending ash floating through the station like swirling snow.

235

Maggie picked up her case, grabbing Alice's hand and pulling her close. Checking the crowded station to make sure Thomas was near, she turned to Mum. A desperate wish to stay burned in her heart with the fear that she would never return home. "Do we have to go?"

"It'll be okay, dear," Mum whispered, pulling her into a tight hug. "We'll see each other soon."

Maggie's lips trembled and she squeezed her eyes shut as she embraced her mother. "I love you, Mum." She couldn't bring herself to say goodbye.

Mum held her for several moments more, then broke away with tears brimming in her eyes. Maggie's heart ached as Alice rushed to clutch her mother, sobbing and refusing to let go. Thomas sniffled as he stared at the train and the platform beside it. Hundreds of families mirrored their situation.

Children pulled away from their mothers.

Families separated.

Everything was falling apart for each of them.

Maggie shuddered and turned towards Mum. "Will Arthur be okay?"

Mum straightened from her hug with Thomas. "Yes." She reached out, straightening the thick cardboard tag pinned to Maggie's coat. "Don't lose it."

"I won't."

"LAST CALL! ALL ABOARD!"

Mum sighed, her hand slipping to Maggie's. "Go on." She kissed Maggie's cheek. "I love you."

Maggie swallowed hard and nodded, grabbing Alice's hand again. "Come on," she whispered.

Smiling at Mum one last time, Maggie led her siblings onto the platform. They followed the flow of children into the train, where they were met by a lady in a dark suit. She led them to a small compartment, pointing out where they could place their luggage. Maggie sat down on the hard bench, pressing her face against the clouded window in hopes of seeing Mum one last time.

But the steam was too thick.

Maggie blinked hard, trying to shove away her tears, and tried to force a smile for her siblings as the train rumbled into the fog.

A hand jostled Maggie's shoulder, shaking her awake. She sat up, stretching. Slowly, her mind caught up to the moment. She and the twins were who knows where, about to be taken to live with a complete stranger.

"Come on, girly," a man with a dark beard and cap stood over her. "It's your stop." Nodding, she reached over to wake the twins.

"Good morning," she said with false cheerfulness. "Time for an adventure?"

Thomas sprang up at those words, blinking away sleep. "Adventure?"

"Yes." Maggie nodded, grabbing their hands and checking for their tags. "A great *big* adventure."

One that I wish didn't have to happen, she added inwardly.

Alice's wide blue eyes searched Maggie's face, and Maggie fought to keep an earnest expression. *Be strong for the twins.*

"Come on, now," the man said, pulling the door open to their crowded compartment. "Everybody off."

Maggie stood, sliding her case under one arm. With the twins in tow, she followed the man out of the train car.

Trembling at the sight of the sea of children, Maggie's heart tore. So many children. And all of them just as terrified and alone as they were.

The station was a storm of people whirling this way and that, their chatter causing a deafening hum. Men and women in dark jackets bustled about, pushing the children against the far wall. "Line up!" a woman snapped.

Maggie blinked.

She clutched her little siblings' hands and pressed her back against the cold stone. The twins huddled next to her, looking like rumpled little Peter-Rabbits with their dark coats and tiny cases.

Suddenly, the commotion stopped. The men and women stepped to the side. Then a new trickle of people appeared. They walked down the line, eyeing the children as they passed.

"We'll take that one." The first couple spoke. They stepped forward, reaching out to the child. The woman smiled kindly, picking up the tiny girl's hand and pulling her away from her grasping older brother. Maggie's eyes widened. They weren't keeping families together? Her pulse sped up, and she pulled her siblings closer. Whatever happened… she couldn't lose the twins.

Minutes that felt like hours went by, and Maggie tried to look as small as she could and hold the twins tightly, avoiding the glances of people walking by.

She was so focused on the grey stone floor that she jumped when voices near her spoke.

"We'll take these two." A young woman stepped forward, reaching towards Alice.

"No!" Maggie jumped forward, throwing her arms in front of her siblings.

The couple stared at her incredulously.

"Is there a problem?" A station agent approached.

Maggie faced him, standing as tall as she could. She tightened her grip on the twins. "We stay together!"

The station agent sighed. "Miss—" he began.

"Please," Maggie whispered.

"We don't have time for this," the young woman snapped. She reached towards Alice's hand. Her husband looked a bit more apologetic.

"We only have room for two." He picked up Thomas's case, giving the boy a smile.

The station agent turned towards Maggie. "I'm sorry, Miss. But if they want them, they have the right to take them."

Maggie fell back against the station wall, stunned.

She watched helplessly through tears as the twins were led away, their small cries of "Maggie!" swallowed by the crowd's din.

One by one, the children were chosen, led away by men and women with sympathy plastered across their faces. One by one the station emptied, but still, Maggie remained. Hot tears pricked her eyes. She had failed the twins… and her mother. She was supposed to be strong for them, but instead she had let them be taken from her.

People continued to file out, and Maggie stood like a statue, loneliness crashing over her.

Piece by piece, everything was falling apart.

The station was nearly empty when a tall, formally dressed man appeared. He walked down the line, leaning slightly on a wooden cane. He stopped before Maggie, gazing at her with gentle grey eyes.

Maggie could barely breathe as he studied her.

"I'll take this one," he finally said in a thick Yorkshire accent.

Butterflies exploded inside her.

Hugging her knees to her chest, Maggie stared at the floral pattern of the thick quilt beneath her. It had been a week since she had moved in with Sir Kendrick, and she felt lonelier than ever. She was well-fed and had everything she needed... but nothing she wanted. She wanted to see her family again.

Dozens of tumultuous feelings rose with a rush of tears

Thomas, Alice, Mum, Arthur...all miles away.

And Daddy... Daddy was completely gone. Never to give her the hug that would fill the aching hole in her heart. He would have kept them together. None of this would have happened if he hadn't...

No, she couldn't think like this.

Her tears turned to heart-wrenching sobs.

The war was out of her control. Out of anyone's control, it seemed.

The war... That was another piece of the world tumbling out of place. News of the new German army had reached even her ears. They seemed set on destroying the world.

How long would it be before she could see her siblings' faces? Feel Mum's embrace again?

How long would it be before everything could be pieced back together?

Slowly, her tears were replaced by an empty ache.

She sniffed, looking around for a handkerchief to wipe her eyes. Her still not-quite-unpacked case lay beside her on the bed, and she undid the clasps with trembling fingers. She fingered through her belongings, and something else white caught her eye.

What's this?

She unfolded the paper, nearly bursting into tears again when she saw familiar handwriting.

Megs,

You know how bad I am at writing things like this. But... I wanted to say how sorry I am. I should never have yelled at you for something that was my fault. It was so very wrong. When you were at school the other day, Mum had me go through our Bible. I found something that I thought you might want to read.

Proverbs 3:5.

Go read it.

I know how easy it is for you to feel like you've lost control— especially now that we don't have Dad to lean on.

Well... you don't need control. The verse will show you how.

I'll miss you when you leave. Hopefully Mum remembers to put this in your case.

– Arthur

Maggie let the letter flutter to her lap. Her loneliness eased, just a little, at the memory of her older brother.

But where can I find a Bible?

She had been briefly shown around the mansion, and she remembered the housekeeper had gestured to a tall double-door and said it was a library.

Maggie could hardly remember where everything was, but it was worth a try. She locked her case with the letter inside and slid off the bed.

As she walked down a long hallway, she noticed Sir Kendrick in his study. His brow was furrowed in concentration as he flipped through a book. She hurried past before he could look up.

Making her way down a wide staircase and across one of the great halls, she found the tall doors.

She slipped between them, only to halt in awe.

Even in this mansion, she had never thought a library could be so *big*.

Towering shelves lined the walls, stuffed full of scarlet, chestnut, and muted-sage hardcovers.

Gilded books lay on side tables, inviting one to sit down in one of the plush settees and read the day away.

Where would she even start?

Stepping over to a side table, she began with the books cluttering its surface. Sure enough, a large leather Bible lay among the others. Hesitantly, she sat down on the adjacent settee and opened it.

Proverbs 3:5.

Flipping through the fragile pages, she stopped.

"Trust in the Lord with all thine heart; and lean not unto thine own understanding."

"Trust in the Lord," she murmured.

What had Arthur meant when he said the verse would help her? Of course she trusted in God.

Do you? A small voice of doubt whispered in her mind.

Maggie blinked hard before reading the words again.

"Lean not unto thine own understanding."

Arthur's letter ran through her mind.

I know how easy it is for you to feel like you've lost control—especially now that we don't have Dad to lean on. Well... you don't need control.

Yes—Daddy was gone, his firm protection removed from their family. Yes—Arthur was hurt, war was waging, and her family was separated.

But…

"Lean not unto thine own understanding."

In her understanding, everything was falling apart.

But what if… What if it wasn't?

Could she place her *true* trust in Him? Lean on Him completely? In everything? Was there a way to feel like everything wasn't torn apart?

Maggie bit her lip, tears dripping down her cheeks. She closed her eyes.

"Lord?"

Maggie sat cross-legged in a wicker chair beside a quiet pond. The cool spring air brushed her face as she fingered the sage green cover of the book cradled in her hands. Ever since Sir Kendrick had gifted her the wonderful hardcover, her days had been a swirl of dragons and dwarves, goblins and elves, mountain kingdoms, and even a magical golden ring. Winter had passed with her barely even noticing.

Over the months, she had grown quite close to the old knight who housed her. Sir Kendrick had learned of her struggle, and—being a Christian himself—had kindly led her through lengthy discussions on trusting in Christ.

Slowly—ever-so-slowly—she was learning to lean on Him.

The thought of time passing turned her thoughts to the time of year.

Suddenly, she jerked up, gasping. The book fell unnoticed from her fingers. Had she really forgotten?

She ran through the days in her mind, assuring

herself that, yes indeed, she had. Today was her birthday.

I'm fourteen!

Maggie sprang up, reaching for the book. She turned towards the mansion, ready to celebrate, before she remembered.

There was no one to celebrate with. Her family was scattered all across England, who-knows where.

She sank down, her spirit following suit. She was alone.

A tear trickled down her face.

No.

Maggie took a deep breath. She wasn't alone. *He* was with her. She could celebrate her birthday and know the Lord would take care of her family.

She just had to remember that He was with her in everything.

Brushing the tears from her eyes, Maggie took another breath. Just as she was about to open her book again, she heard a noise.

A high-pitched voice whispered behind her, quickly *shushed* by a deeper one. She frowned, confused, and started to turn around. She hardly had time to blink before two small figures crashed into her

"*Surprise!*" one shrieked.

Maggie fell back onto the grass, her mouth falling open.

Alice sprang up, diving at her in another hug. Thomas followed, and the reality of the situation dawned on Maggie, filling her with sudden joy.

"How... How did you get here?" Maggie gasped, wrapping her arms around her sister. She felt like she was in the most perfect dream.

"Did we surprise you?" Thomas laughed, dancing in

a circle.

Maggie nodded, unable to find words, her eyes wide.

Alice lifted her head, her bright eyes laughing through her light brown curls. "See!?" she cried, looking behind Maggie, "I said we could!" She looked back at Maggie. "He said we wouldn't!"

A groaning laugh sounded behind them.

Who said? Maggie tried to turn and see who was back there, but the twins grabbed her arms. "And we have another surprise!" Thomas cried gleefully, tugging at her.

Maggie staggered to her feet. "What?" she laughed, brushing her mussed hair out of her eyes. A voice spoke behind her.

A familiar voice, one that she had longed to hear for months.

"Happy Birthday, Megs."

Maggie gasped, dropping the twins' hands and spinning around. Only one person called her that. Arthur stood before her, a wide grin lighting up his face.

Maggie's jaw dropped.

After the twins, the fact that he was here wasn't the most astounding.

But...he was... *standing.* Two wooden crutches supported him, and even though he wobbled slightly on his one leg, he was *standing.*

Maggie's hands flew to her mouth.

"Surprised?" Arthur laughed.

Maggie flew to him, burying her head in his shoulder. Joyful tears soaked her cheeks.

Arthur wrapped his arms tightly around her.

"Happy Birthday, Megs," he whispered again.

The End

ABOUT THE AUTHORS

Jae Fisher, a college student, lives in her hometown in Upstate South Carolina with her family surrounding her. When she yearns for inspiration, Jae goes about her job at a local restaurant with a book in hand. Some yellow pad paper and pen are always in her hands with a handwritten version of her future novel, *The Dares Chronicles.*
Connect with Jae: instagram.com/the_sapphire_writer

Bree Pembrook is a fifteen-year-old homeschooled, barefoot loving, crazy Christian who loves writing, family, reading, exploring the forest, listening to music, and being with friends. She lives in a place somewhere with her three sisters, three brothers, and two incredible parents.
Connect with Bree: laughsandliterature.wordpress.com

Analise M. Martin is an Anabaptist writer who seeks to live as she writes: passionately, without fear, and in love with the Author who created her. When not writing, she is usually trying to learn something new. Sometimes she even succeeds! Her hobbies at present include reading excessively, trying all manner of artistic ideas, and keeping a Commonplace book.
Connect with Analise: elfenstaubauthornewsletter1344.ck.page

P.D. Atkerson is a homeschooled writer living in Montana. She spends almost as much time in the worlds she creates as she does the real one. When she's not reporting the stories of her agents, she's making cakes, learning different languages, or traveling to different worlds through the portals of books.

She has a black belt in sarcasm and a master's degree in useless facts.

Connect with P.D.: pdatkerson.com

Elisabeth Joy is a master obfuscator, an incurable daydreamer, a self-proclaimed crazy homeschooler, and a writer at heart. As a wallflower, she notices many things that others miss and has a habit of intertwining the stories she sees into the stories she spins.

Connect with Elisabeth: agentstormhawk.wixsite.com/isasmile

Sandralena Hanley spent her childhood making up stories and illustrating them. She is the author of an epic Christian fantasy series, the Valdeor Chronicles. She lives in beautiful northern Idaho with her husband. Her hobbies are painting, reading, writing, and dreaming up imaginary worlds.

Connect with Sandralena: sandralenahanley.com

E. N. Leonard is a traveler who loves mountains and forests wherever she can find them. Her passion for reading, creativity, and ideas started with art and poetry, and when God put a story in her lap, she flung herself into the wonderful world of writing. There are no reports of her return. She also enjoys studying homeopathy, learning languages, singing in the woods, and playing with her dog.

Connect with E. N.: writesy-artist-ramblings.ck.page

Bethany Willcock is a Christian homeschool grad with a passion for coffee, cats, piano, and all things vintage. She runs a home bakery and spends most of her spare time reading, researching, and writing historical and contemporary mysteries.

Connect with Bethany: goodreads.com/bethanywillcock

ABOUT THE AUTHORS

Katja H. Labonté is a Christian, an extreme bibliophile who devours over 365 books in a year, and an exuberant writer with a talent for starting short stories that explode into book series. She is a bilingual French-Canadian and has about a dozen topics she's excessively passionate about (hint: that's why she writes). She spends her days enjoying little things, growing in faith, learning life, and loving people.
Connect with Katja: littleblossomsforjesus.wordpress.com

Lilly Wiscaver is a homeschool graduate, a participant in the National Bible Bee, a photographer, and most importantly, a follower of Christ. She loves memorizing the Bible, reading, writing, and working on various sewing projects. She enjoys working on an organic farm and loves learning about herbalism from a Christian worldview.
Connect with Lilly: adaughterservingtheking.wordpress.com

Erika Mathews writes Christian living books, both fiction and non-fiction, that demonstrate the power of God in ordinary people, transforming daily life into His resting life. The author of the kingdom adventure fiction series *Truth from Taerna,* she's passionate about encouraging others to intimately know Jesus. She enjoys playing with her children, reading, editing, anything outdoors, being organized, oceans, lakes, autumn, and sunrises.
Connect with Erika: restinglife.com

Rebekah A. Morris is a homeschool graduate, an enthusiastic freelance author, and a passionate writing teacher. Her books include, among others, *Home Fires of the Great War, The Unexpected Request, Gift from the Storm,* and her best-selling *Triple Creek Ranch* series. Some of her favorite pastimes, when she isn't writing, include reading and coming up with dramatic and original things to do. The Show-Me state is where she calls home.

Connect with Rebekah: readanotherpage.com

A. F. Kopp is a twenty-one-year-old writer with a love for crafting relatable and eye-opening stories. Whether through sweet protagonists (or totally unreliable ones), Kopp tries to bring readers into a world only to broaden the scope of what life can truly mean through meaningful relationships, redemption, and an understanding of one's faith.

Connect with A.F.: afkoppauthor.com

Hannah E. Griggs is a teacher and author of primarily middle-grade Christian fiction. She loves graphic design, history, and coffee. When she's not writing, you'll find her building her education business, reading Christian fiction and biographies, or improving her guitar skills in her home in Texas.

Connect with Hannah: hannahegriggs.com

Autumn Nicole is a teen girl with a deep love for Jesus, her family, and powerful stories. She's a farm girl, budding florist, homeschool graduate, aspiring author, and sister to eleven. You can usually find her in the greenhouse or fields, and in her spare time she loves dabbling in photography, scrapbooking memories, cuddling babies, enjoying the sunshine, reading the Bible, laughing with her siblings, and eating oreos.

Connect with Autumn: ibelieveevenwhen.wordpress.com

Bethany Griggs is a blogger of Christian simple living and author of Christian contemporary fiction. She enjoys crafts from paper, coziness, and creativity. Oh, and alliteration! As

someone with multiple chronic illnesses, she loves encouraging people through the rough places, rejoicing with them in the good ones, and pointing them to Jesus her Savior.
Connect with Bethany: arubyintherough.com

An avid reader and incurable story-spinner, **Angie Thompson** also enjoys volunteering in her church's children's program and starting (but not always finishing) various kinds of craft projects. She currently lives in central Virginia near most of her incredible family, including two parents, six brothers, one sister, and five siblings-in-law—plus four nieces, ten nephews, and several assorted pets!
Connect with Angie: quietwaterspress.com

Cassie Creley is a writer and blogger living in the Pacific Northwest. Eight of her poems have been published in literary journals. Cassie's favorite plants to grow in her garden are hydrangeas, dahlias, zucchinis, and strawberries. She loves being able to connect with and interview others living with chronic health conditions like POTS, fibromyalgia, and ME/CFS. She blogs about creativity, faith, and finding joy in chronic illness.
Connect with Cassie: cassiecreley.com

A. Y. Daniels is a young writer with a heart for exciting, sweet, and encouraging stories. She longs to please her Savior with her writing. Known as Vonnie by her friends, she loves Jesus, her family and friends, horses, writing, and artwork. If she isn't writing or doing school, she's either chatting with her friends, procrastinating cleaning, or playing with cover design.
Connect with A. Y. Daniels: thejourneytowrite.wordpress.com

Sherrice Myers is a math teacher in a Christian school. She does writing part time but would love for it to become more than just a hobby. She loves all things coffee and enjoys spending her free time curled up with a fuzzy blanket, a warm drink, and her current work in progress.

Connect with Sherrice: penlightenment.quest

Alaina Johnson is an artist, fangirl, and writer of complex, fantastical tales who hails from the great state of North Dakota. She loves Jesus, drawing, movies, blankets, and cookies. When she's not staring at the vast whiteness of her computer document, you'll find her listening to music, daydreaming, or reading speculative fiction. Throughout her writing, she weaves stories of broken characters who strive to cling to hope amid the darkness.

Lucy Peterson is a young North Dakota prairie girl with an unquenchable fountain of stories flowing through her head. She's convinced she was born into the wrong world and will dig through every wardrobe and try on every golden ring she meets. She is an Imagineer, Elf Maiden, and Narnian queen at heart, and strives in all her writing to bring glory to the One True King.

Connect with Lucy: luluslibrary.com

Find out more about The King's Daughters Writing Camp at
kingsdaughterswritingcamp.com